ALREADY

DEAD

(A Laura Frost Suspense Thriller —Book Five)

BLAKE PIERCE

Blake Pierce

Blake Pierce is the USA Today bestselling author of the RILEY PAGE mystery series, which includes seventeen books. Blake Pierce is also the author of the MACKENZIE WHITE mystery series, comprising fourteen books; of the AVERY BLACK mystery series, comprising six books; of the KERI LOCKE mystery series, comprising five books; of the MAKING OF RILEY PAIGE mystery series, comprising six books; of the KATE WISE mystery series, comprising seven books; of the CHLOE FINE psychological suspense mystery, comprising six books; of the JESSE HUNT psychological suspense thriller series, comprising nineteen books; of the AU PAIR psychological suspense thriller series, comprising three books; of the ZOE PRIME mystery series, comprising six books; of the ADELE SHARP mystery series, comprising thirteen books, of the EUROPEAN VOYAGE cozy mystery series, comprising four books; of the new LAURA FROST FBI suspense thriller, comprising six books (and counting); of the new ELLA DARK FBI suspense thriller, comprising nine books (and counting); of the A YEAR IN EUROPE cozy mystery series, comprising nine books, of the AVA GOLD mystery series, comprising six books (and counting); and of the RACHEL GIFT mystery series, comprising six books (and counting).

An avid reader and lifelong fan of the mystery and thriller genres, Blake loves to hear from you, so please feel free to visit www.blakepierceauthor.com to learn more and stay in touch.

BOOKS BY BLAKE PIERCE

RACHEL GIFT MYSTERY SERIES
HER LAST WISH (Book #1)
HER LAST CHANCE (Book #2)
HER LAST HOPE (Book #3)
HER LAST FEAR (Book #4)
HER LAST CHOICE (Book #5)
HER LAST BREATH (Book #6)

AVA GOLD MYSTERY SERIES
CITY OF PREY (Book #1)
CITY OF FEAR (Book #2)
CITY OF BONES (Book #3)
CITY OF GHOSTS (Book #4)
CITY OF DEATH (Book #5)
CITY OF VICE (Book #6)

A YEAR IN EUROPE
A MURDER IN PARIS (Book #1)
DEATH IN FLORENCE (Book #2)
VENGEANCE IN VIENNA (Book #3)
A FATALITY IN SPAIN (Book #4)

ELLA DARK FBI SUSPENSE THRILLER
GIRL, ALONE (Book #1)
GIRL, TAKEN (Book #2)
GIRL, HUNTED (Book #3)
GIRL, SILENCED (Book #4)
GIRL, VANISHED (Book 5)
GIRL ERASED (Book #6)
GIRL, FORSAKEN (Book #7)
GIRL, TRAPPED (Book #8)
GIRL, EXPENDABLE (Book #9)

LAURA FROST FBI SUSPENSE THRILLER
ALREADY GONE (Book #1)
ALREADY SEEN (Book #2)

WATCHING (Book #1)
WAITING (Book #2)
LURING (Book #3)
TAKING (Book #4)
STALKING (Book #5)
KILLING (Book #6)

RILEY PAIGE MYSTERY SERIES
ONCE GONE (Book #1)
ONCE TAKEN (Book #2)
ONCE CRAVED (Book #3)
ONCE LURED (Book #4)
ONCE HUNTED (Book #5)
ONCE PINED (Book #6)
ONCE FORSAKEN (Book #7)
ONCE COLD (Book #8)
ONCE STALKED (Book #9)
ONCE LOST (Book #10)
ONCE BURIED (Book #11)
ONCE BOUND (Book #12)
ONCE TRAPPED (Book #13)
ONCE DORMANT (Book #14)
ONCE SHUNNED (Book #15)
ONCE MISSED (Book #16)
ONCE CHOSEN (Book #17)

MACKENZIE WHITE MYSTERY SERIES
BEFORE HE KILLS (Book #1)
BEFORE HE SEES (Book #2)
BEFORE HE COVETS (Book #3)
BEFORE HE TAKES (Book #4)
BEFORE HE NEEDS (Book #5)
BEFORE HE FEELS (Book #6)
BEFORE HE SINS (Book #7)
BEFORE HE HUNTS (Book #8)
BEFORE HE PREYS (Book #9)
BEFORE HE LONGS (Book #10)
BEFORE HE LAPSES (Book #11)
BEFORE HE ENVIES (Book #12)
BEFORE HE STALKS (Book #13)

BEFORE HE HARMS (Book #14)

CHAPTER ONE

Detective Scott Waters jumped out of the car while the engine was still running, leaving his partner cursing behind him. He didn't want to wait. He was always being told he was too impatient, but what else was he supposed to do when someone's life was on the line?

He darted down the street towards the opening of the alleyway, where he could already see a man standing slumped against the wall, his head down. He looked up at the sight of a police officer running towards him and straightened, pointing wordlessly, with a pale face and one single outstretched finger, down the alley.

Scott nodded at him without breaking stride, skidding around the corner and then coming to a complete halt. It was pretty clear that they were too late to make a difference.

Scott cursed mentally, wanting to hit the wall with his fist but very aware that he was being watched by a member of the public. When he'd heard the call over the radio, that someone had found Evelina Collins and she looked like she'd been attacked, he'd been hopeful that the person got it slightly wrong. That she was still alive and could be saved. They'd all been hoping that she would turn up alive from the moment she was reported missing.

But, this…

There was no mistaking it.

Evelina was dead, and maybe long dead. Scott stared at her neck, the way it gaped open like some kind of cartoonish second smile. It didn't even look real. He hadn't seen many bodies, working out here in Pacific Cove. Murders didn't happen often here.

Still, he knew it was real.

He reached for his radio to call it in, wishing he hadn't run out ahead of his partner. This was weird, and he had no idea what he was supposed to do.

"Waters?"

Scott turned slightly as his partner finally caught up, coming to a stop beside him. "What the hell are we supposed to do with that, Davis?"

1

Davis stared at the scene in front of them, looking just as confused as Scott felt. "Uh... I don't know. Bag it up as evidence?"

"How are we supposed to bag a flame?" Scott asked. "You can't put a burning candle in an evidence bag."

"Right," Davis agreed. They both stared down at it a moment longer. The candle was set right in the middle of Evelina's chest, her dead, pale hands holding it in place like some kind of morbid recreation of a funeral pose. Not that funeral poses weren't morbid in the first place. It was slowly going down, wax melting and dripping down the candle to pool on her chest. "Well, maybe we let it burn out and then put it in an evidence bag."

"Isn't it..." Scott gestured vaguely. "I don't know. Contaminating the scene? What if there's evidence on her hands or her clothes?"

"Then blow it out!" Davis said, with renewed urgency, motioning his younger partner forward.

Scott sprang a step ahead, then realized he was going to have to get down on his knees next to Evelina to reach it. He dropped quickly, trying not to touch anything, and blew quickly until the flame went out. Then he breathed for a second, and the smell hit him: the sickly-sweet tang of blood, the scent of death, something unique and undefinable. Nothing else smelled quite like it.

He turned quickly to take a breath of the air flowing in off the seafront and into the alley, so he wouldn't throw up.

"What does it mean?" Davis asked, still standing safely far away to avoid inhaling anything himself. Scott looked up at him, glanced over the body one more time, and then stood up.

"I don't know," he said. "But I've never heard anything like it. We better call it in."

"Right," Davis said, reaching for his radio instead this time. "I'll get the chief down here. I think we need someone with a bit more experience on this one."

Scott said nothing as Davis stepped away to make the call, covering a hand over his own radio as it spit out the same words. He was looking down at Evelina, at the wax still cooling on her hands.

He had a very bad feeling about that candle – about it maybe not being the only one they were going to find.

CHAPTER TWO

Laura had to stop and give herself a moment as she poured Lacey another glass of juice, standing in her kitchen like it was nothing. Looking over at the little blonde girl playing on the floor, she almost had to pinch herself.

Her daughter was here. Playing with her toys. Doing normal kid things. And she had been here all weekend.

It was the third weekend in a row that Lacey had stayed over, since Laura had gained that right at the custody hearing. And even though it was starting to feel completely normal, there were still moments when she had to remind herself it was *real*.

"Here you go, sweetie," Laura said, carrying the glass over to her. "We'll get ready in a little while, okay? I don't want to be late."

"Can I bring all my cats?" Lacey asked, gesturing to the fluffy toys she was currently pretending to brush and dress up with Velcro bows. "Amy said she wanted to see them."

"Of course, you can," Laura said, smiling. She sat down on the sofa behind Lacey, reaching for her own cup of coffee from the table. "So long as you promise to pack them all away when it's time to go. We don't want to keep Daddy waiting."

Lacey pouted slightly, then shuffled backwards across the floor to lean against her mother's legs. She was still wearing her pajamas, a matching pink set which declared her to be 'Daddy's little angel.' Laura was sure her ex-husband, Marcus, sent her with that outfit on purpose. Just to try to get a rise out of her.

He couldn't have been further off the mark. Just having Lacey in her life again after going for so long without seeing her meant that Laura was willing to take any insult. Nothing could ruin how happy she felt to get to be a mom again.

"Can't I stay here longer?" she asked. "I don't want to go back yet."

Secretly, Laura was thrilled, and inside her head she was grinning and doing a victory dance. Outwardly, though, she just smiled little and tousled Lacey's hair. "I know, sweetie. I always want the weekend to last forever, too. But you've got to go back to school, remember?"

Lacey sighed and rolled her eyes in that way that only a six-year-old could, full of sass that seemed too grown-up and was therefore highly comical. "Ughhhh. I don't want to go to school. I want to stay with you!"

Laura hid another smile behind her coffee cup. "School's really important, Lacey. And anyway, don't you want to go see your friends?"

"I could play with Amy instead," Lacey pointed out.

Laura chuckled, shaking her head. "Come on, you. Time to get dressed and go see your new favorite person. You get to play with her today, and tomorrow she has to go to school as well, okay? The quicker we get ready, the more time you'll have to show her your cats."

This promise sent Lacey rocketing out of the living room and into the small bedroom that she was currently sharing with Laura, with a child-sized bed set up at the foot of Laura's own. It wasn't much, but it was all she had been able to offer. Rent was high enough here in Washington, D.C., as it was, and Laura was still trying to recover financially from her own past mistakes.

As well as in every other way. Not too long ago, this morning coffee would have been laced with something stronger to keep the cold out. Not the literal cold of winter, which was blooming strong outside her windows, but the cold memories of things she'd seen in her visions. Things that no one would ever want to see.

The thought of her visions made her check her cell phone, a habit that was becoming increasingly urgent over the last few days. She'd even started to open her messaging apps just to make sure she hadn't missed a notification. It wasn't like Nate to go quiet for this long.

Ever since she'd seen a vision of him plunging to his death the last time they spoke, Laura had been fearing the worst. That he was already dead. Even though, logically, she knew someone would have told her, she couldn't help but feel the fear surfacing over and over.

Laura sipped the last of her coffee and set the cup down, sighing. Still nothing. It had been two weeks since their last case ended, and all of her messages and calls had gone unanswered. After he didn't show up to work for the usual debrief on their first Monday back at FBI headquarters, Laura had been puzzled. Then worried. Now, she was practically antsy.

Division Chief Rondelle, their direct superior, would only say that Nate was on leave and that he was fine. And for Laura to ask him herself why he wasn't at work. But Nate wouldn't reply to her, and Laura was getting more and more nervous. The last time she'd spoken

4

to him, it had felt as though he believed in her psychic abilities at last – but also that he wasn't happy about it. Like he no longer wanted to know her.

And, unexpectedly, that hurt even more than it had when he hadn't believed her.

"Are you nearly ready?" she called out, knowing that Lacey needed a prompt or two in order to get her moving in the mornings – even when she had the motivation of a playdate.

"Yes, Mom!" Lacey called back at the top of her voice.

Laura hid a smile, knowing this meant her daughter had probably just dropped whatever toy she'd been distracted by and scrambled to actually start dressing herself. She had some time, then. Knowing that her boss was always working, no matter the day or time – she'd never actually seen him not in uniform, and only a handful of times not behind his desk – she dialed his number. If she didn't get answers, this feeling of worry wasn't going to go away. The last thing she needed was another challenge to her sobriety, and legitimate fear over the safety of someone she cared about was a serious challenge.

"Division Chief Rondelle." His voice came over the speakers with the reassuring familiarity of someone who could always be counted on to be the same.

"Chief, it's Laura," she said. "Sorry to call on a weekend."

"Go ahead," he said, with magnanimity. She'd known he would.

"I know you told me to wait or to ask him, but I just… I'm getting worried," Laura said. "It's Nate. Can you at least tell me what kind of leave he's taken? It's not medical, is it?"

Rondelle sighed, and for a heart-lurching moment Laura thought he was going to say that she was right.

"No," he said. "It's not medical leave. Look, Laura, I was going to speak to you about this tomorrow, but I suppose now is as good a time as any."

"What is it?" she asked, her heart pounding with fear. If Rondelle had been planning to set up a meeting and talk to her formally, it was probably serious. But if it wasn't medical, then…

"Agent Lavoie came to me late on Friday and put in a request," Rondelle replied. He paused then, as if he needed a break to approach such a delicate matter. "I'm afraid he wants to transfer to a new partner."

5

Laura's heart sank right down into her feet. If sh
sitting down, she had the feeling she would have]
something for support.

She and Nate had been partners for almost four
closest friend, even if he didn't know it. The persor
count on to have her back. Before him, she'd ha‹
short-term partners, as well as a lot of solo work. It hadn t ᵇᵉ
fulfilling. Having that connection with someone, actually wanting to
work with them day after day – it made all the difference. He'd been
there for her through some of her darkest days – days when she was
stuck at the bottom of a bottle, days when she'd thought she would
never see her daughter again. And going back to not having that…

It would be lonely. So lonely. And she didn't want to lose him.
Even though she immediately knew why he must have put in the
transfer, her heart rebelled.

She'd told him everything, just like he wanted. Confessed the
whole lot. And he was going to turn his back on her now?

"No," she said, a knee-jerk reaction.

Rondelle made a funny noise, something that could have been a
wry chuckle, wrenched out of him but not from a place of real humor.
"I'm afraid it's not up to you, Laura. Nathaniel has the prerogative to
request a transfer if he so wishes."

"I…" Laura paused, closing her eyes and shaking her head. She
knew. She knew that the protocol dictated he could ask for a transfer
whenever he wanted, and so long as he provided a good enough reason,
Rondelle would give it to him. And Nate was smart. He was an FBI
agent, after all. He wouldn't have put in for a transfer if he hadn't first
thought up a good enough reason.

"I know this is a lot to take in," Rondelle said, with regret in his
voice. "You've been partnered for a while now. But I don't have any
intention of turning down such a reasonable request. We'll talk more
about this tomorrow."

"Alright," Laura said, her mouth dry. What else could she say? She
could scream, shout, cry, and beg, but it would make no difference.
Like Rondelle said, if the request was reasonable, there was no reason
not to grant it.

Unless she could come up with one.

Rondelle ended the call, and Laura looked up to see Lacey
emerging from the bedroom in a getup that put a smile back on her

6

en if it was a sad one: a pink unicorn onesie, complete with a skirt placed over the top.

"I'm a unicorn ballerina," Lacey declared.

"Nice try, kiddo," Laura said, then sighed. If it made her daughter happy, why stop her? It wasn't like they were going out somewhere that she'd be embarrassed by it, and it wasn't a school day. They were just going to spend time with friends. Besides, the fluffy onesie was probably more weather-appropriate than anything else Lacey had brought with her. She shook her head, mostly at her own first instinct to tell Lacey to change. "Oh, fine. You're a unicorn ballerina. Let's go see Amy, shall we?"

"Yeah!" Lacey cheered, her face lighting up with a huge grin. That was enough reward in itself.

Laura reached out to take her by the hand, and they began to file out of the apartment together. But then Lacey stopped by the door, pouting and fidgeting.

"Do you need to pee first?" Laura suggested.

"Yeah," Lacey admitted, then turned and ran for the bathroom.

Laura waited by the door, looking at her cell phone again. He wouldn't answer, would he…?

There was only one way to find out. She dialed Nate's number. Putting the phone to her ear, she listened to it ring until it hit voicemail. She ended the call with a sigh, listening to the sound of the toilet flushing further into the apartment.

"Don't forget to wash your hands," she yelled, hearing Lacey's footsteps quickly retreat from the bathroom door and turn back to the sink before the taps turned on.

Nate wasn't going to talk to her about this. She was going to have to find some way to contact him, to make him see that this wasn't right. They were good together. They worked so well as a team. He couldn't throw that away because he was freaked out by her abilities.

Even if she had to pretend for the rest of their careers that she wasn't psychic after all, it would be worth it to keep him as a partner.

Lacey emerged from the bathroom with that sheepish grin that only a kid who knows they were caught can wear. Laura held a hand out towards her again, prompting Lacey to rush forward and take it. "Come on, trouble," Laura said, smiling at her until it felt real. She had other things to focus on before tomorrow. These weekends with her daughter were fleeting, and she didn't want to waste them preoccupied with work. "Let's go see Amy and Chris."

CHAPTER THREE

Laura retreated to the large open-plan kitchen for a moment of peace, finding Christopher Fallow already setting up the coffee machine for a fresh cup.

"They're having a lot of fun," she said, smiling as she leaned on the marble countertop of the island, waiting for him to finish his preparations.

There was a whirring noise and Chris turned, smiling back at her. He was dressed in a white linen shirt today, the sleeves rolled up over tanned arms, setting off his dark hair and straight, white teeth. She thought, and not for the first time, that he was a handsome man when he smiled. He didn't look anything like his brother. That thought chilled her for a moment, making her remember who Chris was – who he was related to. A monster. "Maybe too much fun," he said with a chuckle. "One day I swear they're going to refuse to separate and we're going to have to start co-parenting."

Laura shook her head at the joke, returning the chuckle. "Remember when you were a kid, and you could make a new best friend in two weeks flat? What happened to that?"

"Oh, I don't know," Chris said. He turned to grab the pot as the coffee machine went silent, pouring out two cups. "I think I get a pretty good first impression when it comes to some people. Enough to know I definitely want them around." He placed one of the cups in front of her, black – just the way she liked it – and met her eyes for just a moment. There was a look in them that sent a thrill along her spine, just for a moment.

What was all that about?

"It's nice for them to bond like this," Laura said. She gestured towards where the girls were playing in Chris' living room, visible from where they stood – and definitely audible. They were concocting some kind of complex storyline involving Lacey's toy cats and Amy's toy ponies, and how their two societies lived together in some strange world. "They've both been through enough to need it. Amy more so, but still."

Chris sipped his coffee, shooting her a look that said he was testing the waters, unsure of how she would respond. "You said you were divorced?"

"Yeah." Laura took a breath, looking down into her coffee. The coffee couldn't look back and judge her. "It's been a tough few years. I was... I'm an alcoholic."

It hurt to say it out loud, almost physically so. Still. After all this time. But then, Laura's recovery hadn't been that long, realistically. She'd been going to the meetings since Marcus handed her the divorce papers, but they hadn't always stuck. She'd fallen off the wagon more than enough times in the years since.

She truly believed the only reason this latest time had been going so well was because she'd known the custody hearing was coming up. Getting her daughter back was powerful motivation, and it had worked. But in the back of her mind, Laura knew that temptation was always going to be there.

"I'm sorry to hear that," Chris said, then made a funny noise in his throat and corrected himself. "Sorry, that sounded like someone died. What I mean is, I'm sorry to hear you've had a tough time. I know people don't just become alcoholics by choice. You must have been through some things."

"Not enough to justify it," Laura said. She took a sip of her coffee to distract herself, to dilute the emotions that came with this topic a little. "Anyway, things went bad between us. Lacey was caught in the crossfire. Until recently, I hadn't even seen her for a long time."

"What changed?" Chris asked. He was looking at her with a kind of open curiosity, an expression that said he just wanted to know more. Not judging her. That made her feel better.

"We had a custody hearing," Laura said. "I get Lacey on weekends, now. It's been a long road to get here."

Chris shifted, turning to face her fully rather than leaning on the counter beside her. "You only get her for weekends? And you're spending them with us?"

Laura looked at him, surprised to see that he actually looked dismayed. "She likes Amy," she said. "And, anyway, I... I don't know. I feel kind of responsible for her, too. In a strange way, I..." She stopped, cutting herself off. Some things felt too raw to say. Besides, she didn't know how Chris would take it.

"You feel kind of like a mom to her, too?" Chris said, softly.

9

Laura darted a glance at him, before looking back at Amy again. He didn't seem upset. "Is that crass to say? She only lost her actual Mom so recently, and I know you were family..."

"No," Chris said, shaking his head and leaning on the counter again. There was emotion underpinning his voice, but he didn't seem upset with her. More upset with the situation in general, the tragedy that Amy had to go through. Having her own father beat her mother to death, only to turn on her next. If Laura hadn't shown up... she was still having bad dreams in which she didn't get there in time. "No, it's kind of reassuring, actually. I'm doing my best, but I know I'm only her uncle. The more people she has looking out for her, the better. And I'm glad you were there. If it wasn't for you sticking your neck out time and time again... I don't know what would have happened to her."

Laura nodded. She took a larger mouthful of her coffee, needing the bitter taste to ground her a little. "I don't like to think about it," she admitted. "She's doing better now. Has she... I mean, with the nighttime situation...?" She kept her words vague, to save both Chris's blushes and Amy's in case the girls overheard. When Chris had reached out to her for help with Amy's bedwetting, his concern had been endearing. And it had been flattering, too, to be the person that he asked.

Chris nodded, giving her a grateful smile. "Your advice was great," he said. "We've had a whole week of dry nights now. I think she might be really settling in at last."

"Just in time for the upheaval of going back to school," Laura commented wryly.

"Yeah," Chris sighed. "I wish I could stay here with her and just... I don't know, homeschool her or something. But the case worker says she'll be better able to adapt and recover the more she has normal socializing situations, and school is perfect for that. And the hospital needs me back."

"You're starting on shift again this week?"

Chris nodded. "Right back in cardiology. It's going to be tough. I've already started to get used to having her around me all day."

"You have childcare options for when she gets out of school?" Laura asked, finding her investigator mode flicking back on, like he'd pressed a switch. "Late shifts, weekends?"

"I've managed to negotiate no weekend shifts for the foreseeable," Chris said. "But, yes, I have childcare. I found someone who can pick her up and take care of her in the afternoons before I get in, and there's a daycare at the hospital in case she has to take time off. She spent some time with Amy earlier in the week, just to get to know each other. I think it's going to work well."

Laura felt an uneasy sensation in the pit of her stomach. What was that? Anxiety?

Jealousy?

She pushed it away, trying not to think about it.

"That's good," she nodded. At least he'd put most of her concerns to rest.

"You know," Chris said, in a conversational tone. "I do hope that one day you'll see me more as a friend, instead of coming over here as an agent."

Laura looked at him sharply, feeling an almost visceral reaction to his unexpected comment. This one she understood fully: guilt. "I, um. I wasn't..." she started, then trailed off. "I'm sorry. I am here as a friend, now. It's just that I'm always going to be concerned she's getting the care she needs. After what happened before, I feel like it's... it's my duty, not just something I care about."

"I understand," Chris said. To her relief, he was smiling. "I'm not trying to give you a hard time. Like I said, I'm glad she has you looking out for her. She needs as many people as she can get."

"Right," Laura said. "So, friends?"

Chris shot her a look that was utterly charming: a smile, a knowing little nod, a dimple in his cheek. "Actually," he said. "Maybe this is a little forward, but I'd like to find out if there might be something more than that."

"More?" Laura repeated, feeling a little stupid even as she said it. *Way to go, Laura. A guy makes a subtle hint that he might like to maybe date you, and you just... parrot his words back to him like you don't understand? Smooth. Really smooth.*

"If you're interested in trying," Chris said. He glanced at where Lacey and Amy were playing, apparently making sure that they weren't listening. "I'd like to take you out to dinner. Maybe some time this week? It would give me a chance to see how Amy does with her new nanny if I'm out of the house for a longer day, too."

For a moment, she was still struck dumb. Chris Fallow. He wasn't his brother, John, but he was close enough. Laura had only wanted to get to know him in the first place to keep an eye on him, to make sure that he wasn't as abusive to Amy as John had been. To keep the little girl safe.

11

But she did seem safe, didn't she? And Chris did seem like a good person.

And if he was fooling her just as well as the former Governor John Fallow had fooled the public, then at least getting closer to him would put her in a better position to find out.

Laura recovered her senses enough to tease him, just a little. "Is that the only reason?"

"No," Chris said, his dimples showing again as he smiled, almost looking like he was about to blush. "No, I've enjoyed getting to know you a little these past few weeks. I'd just like to do that a little more. Maybe in a setting where we can focus on each other, and not the kids."

"Alright," Laura said, nodding and smiling. She had a funny feeling bubbling up inside of her, something she hadn't felt in a long time. That excitement that came along with a new romance. It was like being a teenager again, feeling a little bashful, a little shy and awkward. Mostly, excited. "I'd like that, too. Maybe not on the weekend... Tuesday?"

"Good idea," Chris said, he took a sip of his coffee and then set it down on the counter. "If it goes terribly, we'll have the rest of the week to make up a really good excuse for why the girls can't see each other on Sunday."

Laura caught his joking smile and laughed. The tension dissipated, leaving only that excitement in its wake. She looked over at the girls, at how happy they were. It was a good moment.

It didn't last.

Laura felt her cell phone buzzing in her pocket and pulled it out, looking at the caller ID. She frowned when she saw Rondelle's name flashing up. What did he need to tell her, now? Had the transfer already gone through? Had Nate changed his mind?

Was he in danger?

"I have to get this," she said, apologetically, before walking out rapidly into the hall to answer it. "Agent Frost."

"Hi, Laura. I know we just spoke, but I need you to come in now."

"What is it?" Laura asked, biting her lip. "Is Nate...?" She didn't even know how to finish the sentence. Dead? Hurt? Going somewhere really far away? What?

"It's not about Agent Lavoie," Rondelle told her quickly. "It's a case. It's an emergency. We've got some murders happening in a small-town in California, and the local PD is extremely out of their depth. Two bodies already with the same MO, and it's looking like this could spread. I need you there before it gets out of hand."

Laura bit her lip. Behind her, she could hear the girls playing. "Does it have to be right now? I'm... I'm with my daughter."

Rondelle sighed. "I am sorry, Laura. But this is urgent. We need you."

"Right," Laura sighed back, putting a hand over her eyes. "I'll be there as soon as I can get her back to her dad's place."

She ended the call, turning to go back into the kitchen. Chris was watching her walk back in with concern on his features.

"Everything alright?" he said. "I didn't mean to listen, but... you need to take Lacey back home?"

"I've got a case," Laura said, shaking her head in frustration. "Of all the times for something to come up..."

Truthfully, though, she knew she was lucky. Lucky that it hadn't happened before now. Between her psychic abilities, and the way she gelled so well with Nate, they had built up a reputation for being one of the best agent teams out there when it came to homicides – especially pattern homicides that looked to originate from the same killer.

Nate.

Was he even going to be there?

"I can look after Lacey, if you need it," Chris said. "It sounds like you have to get there pretty urgently – you can come pick her up afterwards?"

Laura hesitated. She knew the drill: Rondelle would give her the briefing, tell her when her plane was leaving, and then she'd have some time to get back and sort Lacey out. She might even make the normal handover time instead of having Marcus sneer at her for bringing her back early. It would be a much better option.

But, leaving her with a stranger...

Only, Chris wasn't a stranger. Not anymore. Laura was confident, now, that he was a good guardian for Amy – someone who would never willingly hurt her or put her in danger. The time they'd spent together since he'd taken over her care had shown her that. And Lacey was having a good time, playing with her friend.

It would be a shame to split them up early, wouldn't it? Especially if they were in good hands already.

"Alright," Laura said, gratefully. "Thank you. I'll be back as soon as I can."

13

Chris nodded. "Don't rush too much," he said. "We need you back here in one piece, and I know the traffic can be heavy getting into the city and back. They'll be fine. I'll make them some food while you're gone, so Lacey will be ready to head home."

Laura nodded. "Thanks," she repeated. "I'll..."

"Just go," Chris said, smiling at her. "Honestly, you don't need to worry. I'll call you the second anything happens, if it does."

Laura nodded again, slowly backing out towards the hall. "Lacey," she said, pausing by the living room door. "Honey, I've just got to pop out for a bit and run an errand. Will you be okay staying here with Chris and Amy?"

Lacey didn't even look up from the game they were playing. "Yes, Mommy!" she called out.

Laura bit her lip, took one last look, then turned for the door.

Time to be an FBI agent again, instead of a mom.

She wondered if this was ever not going to feel like a wrench, to walk away to do her duty and leave Lacey behind.

CHAPTER FOUR

Laura walked in through the open door of Rondelle's office and stopped dead, starting to backtrack.

"Sorry," she said. "I didn't realize you were talking to someone else. I'll wait outside."

"No, no," Rondelle said, getting up from behind his desk. The small, wiry frame of the man belied the power he wielded, not just from his position within the Bureau but also from his natural aura. He had a way of getting people to listen, part of that being the fact he was so sharp he never missed a beat. He always saw when something was going on behind the surface, which made you feel you had to be on your best behavior around him. "Stay, Laura. This is Agent Won."

"Hi," the other man in the room said, turning to extend a hand towards her. He was young, perhaps in his mid-twenties, an Asian-American with shiny dark hair swept back from his forehead. She could see where, if he let it grow out a little longer, it might have natural waves. "Eric, please."

"Hi," Laura replied, out of habit, shaking his hand. She glanced at Rondelle uncertainly. What was this? Some new kid who was training, shadowing Rondelle or something?

"Agent Won will be going with you to Pacific Cove," Rondelle said, which immediately set off alarm bells ringing in Laura's head.

"Uh," she said, glancing around. There was no one else in the room. No sign of Nate. "Does Nate know about this already?"

A fleeting expression passed over Rondelle's face before he tamped it down. But she saw it.

It was pity.

"Agent Lavoie is on leave for the moment," Rondelle said. "He's requested to stay on leave until after his transfer goes through. But Agent Won is a recent graduate from the academy, and while he's worked a few cases, I think he'll really benefit from your expertise. You can show him how our top agents work."

A spasm of pain hit Laura right in the chest. He wasn't even going to see her? Not work with her until it was done? Just go without saying a word?

It occurred to her that until now, Laura had been picturing a scenario in which she was still in contact with Nate. Even if he partnered up with someone else, it might only be temporary. And even if it wasn't temporary, she would still see him around the office. All the agents had desks downstairs. She'd see him there.

Unless, as it now occurred to her, he was transferring out of state. He could easily go work somewhere else. Maybe take up a training role in Virginia, for example.

And he wouldn't have to see her ever again. Meanwhile, she'd be stuck with...

Laura looked at Eric Won in horror. Her new partner. That was what this was, wasn't it? Eric was supposed to be her new partner.

The kid smiled back at her, with bright and wide eyes, as if she was supposed to be excited about getting to work with him.

"As I was saying, the location is Pacific Cove, California," Rondelle said, apparently picking up on her apprehension but wanting to plough through it. "It's a small town, not used to cases like this at all. The locals are swamped already, and once the press starts to head down there in real numbers, they'll be painfully out of their depth. We want to get this killer headed off quickly – he's bold, and we don't want him to get bolder, which is why I'm sending you instead of someone based closer. We've got a couple of bodies so far, but the MO is similar and distinctive enough that they've reached out for help. It's a bit of an odd one. Both bodies were left in public spaces, with candles burning on their chests – still lit by the time local law enforcement was on the scene."

"What's the timeline?" Eric asked, his voice eager. Like a kid who wanted to make sure the teacher noticed him.

"We had two bodies in four nights," Rondelle said. "One last night, and the other on Thursday. By the time you get there, you're going to have about twelve hours to make some progress before we would expect another body. No pressure."

"Nothing like diving in at the deep end," Eric said, with the kind of eager relish that made Laura think they were almost certainly going to have some problems. He was green, anyone could see that. Wanted to prove himself.

Laura didn't need this – not right now. She would have much rather worked the case on her own. She would have said as much, but Rondelle was giving her this knowing look like he knew what she was thinking, and the answer was no.

16

And then she registered what he'd said.

"We're not going right now?" she said, checking her watch.

"I do actually listen to my agents from time to time," Rondelle said. "I know you have Lacey on the weekends now. So, I'm giving you a bit of time to get her away to her father's. Once you add in that delay, you wouldn't be able to get there until the middle of the night, and I'd rather have you both arriving fresh and rested. You're on a four AM flight. Get some sleep before then and be ready to hit the ground running. You'll need to be sharp for this one."

"Briefing notes?" Laura asked, wearily. The whole idea was already exhausting her. She could see everything she needed to do stretching out like a map ahead of her: get back to Chris's place, pick up Lacey, get her home and feed her dinner, pack up her things, take her back to Marcus, pack up her own things, get a few hours of sleep, get to the airport. And then deal with this young pup of an agent who was doubtless going to have far too much energy and enthusiasm, all the while worrying about Nate. And then there was the issue of having to conceal her abilities all over again, just when she was starting to get used to being a little more open. Or, at least, not hiding them.

Rondelle held up a file, and Agent Won eagerly stepped forward to take it. Laura turned to him with a glare, and he cleared his throat quietly before handing it over. She took it without a word. She was the senior agent, by quite some distance. He was going to have to get used to that.

"Play nice," Rondelle said, which Laura took to be his way of dismissing them.

"Yes, sir," she said, though she let just enough sarcasm creep into her voice to let him know what she thought of the whole situation. Not enough to be accused of insubordination, of course. But she knew that he would catch it and know how she felt.

Not that it made a lot of difference.

"I'll see you at the airport, then, Agent Frost?" Agent Won said, as they walked out of Rondelle's office together.

"You will," Laura replied, sweeping ahead of him down the hall. She had to rush now, get everything taken care of.

And if this new kid was expecting to have his hand held through a case like this, then he had another think coming.

***

17

The sound of a scream had Laura running toward the house, all of her busy thoughts thrown out of the window as she raced up the path and grabbed the door handle. It gave way – apparently, Chris didn't bother locking his front door – and she sprinted inside, looking around wildly for her daughter.

She'd been such an idiot. Why had she left Lacey alone with him? His brother was a violent murderer and child abuser, for God's sake! Just because Chris was younger and prettier and had a nice smile, had she really allowed herself to be convinced that he was safe? How could she have forgotten that they grew up in the same household, learned the same values?

"Lacey?" she called out, running in her panic to the last place she had seen the girls – just off the kitchen. But they weren't there.

"Through here!" Chris called out, his voice cheerful and friendly, completely at odds with Laura's panic.

She followed the sound of his voice with a desperate half-sob for air, stumbling into a wide lounge where the girls were sitting on the floor. She caught herself on the threshold, hanging onto the doorframe for support, trying to understand what she saw.

Chris was sitting in an armchair a short distance from them, reading some kind of medical journal with the girls easily in his sights. And the girls themselves, Amy and Lacey both, were smiling and laughing. They had a collection of toy ponies set out in front of them, and as Laura watched, Amy cantered a black horse over towards Lacey's collection of brown ones. Lacey screamed again, then emitted a high-pitched approximation of a neigh, making her ponies run away as a group.

Playing. They were just playing.

Laura looked at Chris again and realized he was watching her with a concerned look, about to drop his journal.

"I… I heard a scream," she said, faintly, feeling a sense of shame wash over her. She'd suspected the worst, just like that. Even though Chris had taken every opportunity to prove to her that he was doing his best. That he wasn't the bad guy. Even though he clearly doted on Amy, and even despite all the ways he'd already proven to her that he was different from his brother.

Chris's face paled a little, and he flapped the pages of the journal to arrange it more neatly in his hands as if her words hadn't affected him at all. "They're alright," he said, off-handedly, but she could hear the hint of strain in his voice. He was disappointed, maybe even hurt, that

18

she'd thought anything could be wrong. "Are you taking Lacey home now?"

"Yes, I am," she said, which made Lacey pout and shake her head crossly. "Sorry, sweetie. We've got to get you back to your dad's, haven't we?"

"But, Mommy," Lacey started, holding up one of the ponies as if she was about to launch into a compelling argument.

"No, sorry," Laura said, cutting her off. "It's your dad's rules, not mine. Come on, love. Let's get your things together and get in the car, okay?"

Chris stood up, putting his journal to one side and standing awkwardly by as Laura helped Lacey on with her coat and made sure she had everything they'd come with. "I'll, um. Still see you later in the week?"

"I hope so," Laura said, but at the look on his face she felt she needed to be more assertive. He looked a little lost, like the ground had dropped from beneath him a bit. Like he needed shoring back up. "Yes. Yes, I'll see you soon."

And she hoped she wasn't a liar, as she led Lacey down the path to the car, ready to load her back to Marcus' place. She wanted to get in, solve this case, and get home. To deal with Nate, to see if things could work with Chris, to focus on her daughter.

In truth, she didn't want to go at all. But duty called, and Laura had never been one to turn down her duty – not when it was something she believed in so strongly.

***

Laura settled into her seat, the familiar yet never quite comfortable shape of the airline chairs embracing her body. She wondered if she was going to have enough time to get a little more shuteye before they got in. It was a six-hour flight. More than enough time for rest.

"Should we go over the briefing notes?" Agent Won asked. Eagerly. Everything he did was eager. He'd greeted her in the airport lounge eagerly. Handed his ticket over to the check-in attendant eagerly. Boarded eagerly.

If he was going to be like this for the whole case, Laura didn't think she would be able to take it.

"Sure," Laura sighed, handing them over to him. "Have at it."

19

"Oh," he said, hesitating with the files still in his hand. "Shouldn't we look at them together?"

Laura knew he was right, obviously. Considering they were working together, yes, they should be looking at the files as a team. But this was too much like going over things with Nate. It was practically a pre-case ritual for them. Settle into the plane and get out the notes for Laura to read out loud to him. Then discuss it before getting a bit of rest, mulling over what they'd read. By the time they hit the ground, they'd have a good idea of where they wanted to start with the investigation.

And this eager little puppy was not Nate. He was *so* not Nate that it was painfully obvious. And given that Nate's absence was like an open wound for her at that moment, the thought of repeating the ritual with this new partner made Laura want to scream.

Anyway, she'd already glanced over them herself. Two young women, killed with cuts to the throat, left with candles in public places. There wasn't anything in the notes yet that stood out to her as an obvious lead. They needed more information, which they could only get on the ground.

"Read them," she said, waving a hand vaguely. "I'll read them after. We can talk about it when we get there – I just want to get some extra sleep. I didn't have enough time for a proper rest before I had to get to the airport."

With that, she pillowed up the FBI-issue standard waterproof jacket she'd brought in her carry-on, put it down on the in-flight table in front of her, set her head down on top of it facing away from Agent Won, and pretended to sleep.

"I just wanted to say," Agent Won began, which made Laura groan internally and open her eyes to look at him balefully. "People around the office were saying that you're some kind of superstar agent, or something. Like, you have this almost supernatural ability to solve murder cases."

"What?" Laura said, sitting up straight. Alarm shot through her veins. She knew people talked about her, obviously. But – *supernatural*? Wasn't that a bit close to the bone?

"Yeah, like, you always get your man," Agent Won said, shrugging. He was annoying her so much already. The informal way he spoke. It felt... untrained. It wasn't that she and Nate were formal with each other, but they spoke in full sentences at least, and could go through a whole conversation without the use of the word 'like'.

God, she sounded like an old woman, didn't she? But she was so unsettled. Knowing Nate had asked for a transfer, having this rookie to babysit, not knowing what to think about her date with Chris, and, of course, having a murderer to catch... She could do without any additional hassle.

"It's just experience," she said, trying to sound bored. "You'll get there one day."

"Oh, I hope I'll be an asset," Agent Won replied. "Maybe I can even help you increase your success rate!"

Oh. So, he wasn't trying to suck up to her. He was trying to brag about how great an agent he was, even though he was freshly baked. How fun.

"I'm going to get some sleep," Laura said again, ignoring his last statement. If she didn't, she would only have something rude to say. She closed her eyes, pillowed her head again, and continued to ignore him as he tried to clear his throat and even say her name, as if she was already so far asleep that she couldn't hear him at all.

She either pretended to sleep, or did sleep, for the better part of six hours.

CHAPTER FIVE

"There," Laura said, pointing ahead of them. There was a police car parked at the side of the road, obvious from its markings and from the way the officer was pacing ahead of it, his hands on his hips. When he saw Laura slowing the car down and pulling up in front of him, he walked towards them, tilting his head to look through the windshield as if trying to identify them.

"Finally," Agent Won said, practically clapping his hands together in glee at this development. "We're here?"

Laura nodded up the road a short way as the officer approached her open window. "GPS says the town boundary is just over there. We're here."

It was a pleasant day, despite it being winter. Next to the cooped-up air of the plane, the fresh breeze coming off the sea was actually refreshing. It was a picturesque part of the California coast, too – down below their car, past a railing, the waves foamed on rocks that looked to have been placed there perfectly by some Hollywood crew. Scrubby trees and dry, old grass indicated that this was probably a lush paradise in the summer, and ahead Laura could see signs for a turning that would take them to a local beach.

Pacific Cove was obviously a nice place to visit all year round, but much nicer when the weather was warm and the flowers were blooming. Laura was already forming a picture in her head of what to expect. A quiet town, much larger than it needed to be, because they were used to large numbers of tourists coming through. Most likely a close community, where everyone knew everyone. That could make their job easier, and it could also make it harder. Rumors could travel fast, and they weren't always accurate.

"Ma'am," the officer said, leaning down to speak to her through the window. He was younger than she'd expected, with sandy-brown hair that seemed to curl in every direction but the one he likely intended when he took off his hat. "I'm Detective Scott Waters with the Pacific Cove PD. Are you the agents we've been expecting?"

"That's right," Laura said, taking her hands off the wheel to reach for her badge. "I'm Special Agent Laura Frost."

"Special Agent Eric Won," Won added quickly, throwing his own badge out in front of Laura so rapidly that she actually had to pull herself back to avoid the danger of being hit with it. "Oh, sorry."

"Our chief asked me to meet you here and escort you wherever you'd like to go first," Detective Waters said. "He felt I could be of the most help to you, as I was the first responder on the scene at both murders."

"Is that so?" Laura asked, lifting an eyebrow. "How big is your police department here?"

"Not big," Waters shrugged. "There's five of us, in all."

Laura nodded. So, a coincidence, then, most likely. If the department had been larger, she might have eyed Waters himself with a lot more suspicion. But since there were so few officers to begin with, the likelihood of the same one finding each of the bodies was a lot higher. Still, it was something to keep in the back of her mind, just in case.

"Let's go to the latest crime scene," Laura said. "You'll lead us there in your car?"

"Yes, ma'am," Waters nodded respectfully. "I'll take you there right now."

He hustled back to his car with a half-run. Laura was pleased, at least, to see a little deference from the locals. Her last case had been something of a nightmare, always butting heads with a Captain who clearly didn't want them there. This one, though, was young and probably in awe of having real-live FBI agents come to his small town. Her seniority here, with Won rather than Nate, might actually be something of a gift.

Not that it made up in any way for not having Nate around.

Laura started the engine up again as the police cruiser in front of them started up, then pulled out after it. They made a solemn procession down the road that led into town, past aesthetically pleasing rock formations, more foamy cliffs, and that beach, covered in soft white sand below them. From there, they wound between quaint little hillside houses, each of them spaced widely apart, and soon entered the town itself.

Pacific Cove was much what Laura had pictured in her mind: old-fashioned white-fronted buildings flanked both sides of the street, still bearing old-style banners and signs as if the town was stuck in a previous century. The stores and businesses were brightened with painted window frames or facades, with jolly stars and stripes bunting and flags hanging from storefronts and lampposts. It was a tourist town. Even the few modern interventions – a nationally-known chain café tucked beside a barber shop, a couple of luxury hotels and a new block of condos – managed to fit in with the overall style of the place.

And Laura didn't fail to notice, too, how people watched when they drove by. Staring at the cop car first, then the fact that another was following it. Word was going to spread that the FBI were in town very fast – and that, too, might end up being the kind of thing that could cause them problems.

"It's beautiful here," Agent Won said, wistfully.

"Hmm," Laura replied, her mind on other things. She had a good idea of where Waters was taking them, and she had a feeling it wasn't going to stay beautiful for very long.

Sure enough, he pulled up suddenly in a spot along the side of the road, clearly an approach to a marketplace. Laura saw the yellow police tape fluttering in the breeze before anything else. This was it.

She got out of the car without comment to Won, figuring he ought to be smart enough to know to follow her if he'd managed to make it through Quantico.

There was a slight possibility that she was being a little unfair, and a much higher one that she was being more unfriendly than Agent Won deserved. It wasn't really his fault that he wasn't Nathaniel Lavoie. But that fact rankled in her throat all the same, and Laura hadn't exactly been given the time required to come to terms with it.

"This is it, up ahead," Detective Waters said, gesturing ahead. He hung back, as if reluctant to go any closer. "She was put there yesterday evening. We got an anonymous tip from a caller who used that payphone right next to it."

Laura took in the position of the payphone, against the wall of a nearby business, glancing around quickly. "No camera footage from around here?"

Waters shook his head no. "There used to be a camera up on the corner, but it got defaced last year by some drunk tourist and they took it down. I guess they were getting around to replacing it, but it just never got done."

Laura nodded. Figured. If it would have been that easy, the locals wouldn't have needed to call the FBI. "So, walk me through it," she said. "You were first on the scene. What did you see?"

"Did you get my briefing notes?" Waters asked, glancing at her almost pleadingly.

"We did," Laura said. Out of the corner of her eye, she saw Agent Won helpfully holding them up with a grin. He was acting like was on vacation, not attending a crime scene. "But I want to hear it from you, now. Paint the picture for me."

Waters swallowed, braced his jaw, then nodded. "So, my partner drove down here, and I was in the passenger seat. We parked about where we're standing now, and we could already see something on the ground, so I got out and rushed ahead." He walked forward a few paces quickly, as if demonstrating. Laura followed him and couldn't help noticing Won copying the same quick paces as if he was literally walking in Waters's footsteps. "As I got around here, I could make out what it was. Ashley."

"Ashley Christianson," Laura said, recalling it from the notes.

"She was a twenty-two-year-old local woman who worked at a diner near here, right?" Agent Won spoke up. Like he was trying to prove he'd read the case notes, too.

"That's right," Waters said, glancing back at him. Laura wished Agent Won would shut up. Waters was obviously battling emotions right now, and she wanted as much of the story from his mouth as she could get. She wanted the raw, visceral reaction of the person who had been on the scene, because that was more valuable than any impression that she could get from the scene herself – especially now that the body had been taken away.

"Where was she?" Laura asked, prompting Waters to get back on track and hoping they hadn't lost too much steam.

"Right here," he said, moving forward and ducking under the tape. It was only a small area that had been marked off, and people were already placing bouquets of flowers all around it. It was a couple of feet from the payphone, right in the center of the street.

Up ahead, market stalls with quaint wooden boards painted with flowers and hand lettering stood empty, no doubt a permanent fixture of this part of town designed to draw in buyers during the tourist season. Right now, their metal frames, devoid of the normal drapes and goods that would pretty them up, seemed almost ominous. The street opened up into a market square which extended towards the shore, making this very obviously a focal point for the town.

"This is extremely public," Laura said. "Was there anyone else around when you found her?"

"No," Waters said. "It was pretty late, so I guess no one had come by here for a while. I was the only person on the scene."

It made sense. That was how the killer had managed to put the body here without being caught. In order to put it down in such a public place, it had to be done under cover of night. A time when everyone else was sleeping. And yet, the candle had been lit – as if drawing attention to her.

"Tell me about the candle," Laura said. "Describe how she was laying."

Waters swallowed again, cleared his throat, and quickly shook his head as if to dislodge something. "Sorry," he said. "I went to school with Ashley, you know? She was a couple years younger than me, but…"

"It's alright, take your time." Laura watched him carefully, how he seemed to be trying to put a professional face back on. Was it real? She thought so, by her gut instinct. So far, Waters was checking out. But she'd been fooled before, and she was going to keep her eye on him for the rest of the case as well.

"She was flat on her back," Waters said. "Fully clothed, and everything. There was blood on her shirt and her chest, where her throat had been cut, but there was no blood on the ground."

"She must have been moved," Won spoke up. The obvious.

Waters nodded, his concentration broken momentarily by the distraction. "Um. The candle… she was kind of holding it in her arms, like this?" He held his own hands across his chest, crossing them and cupping them around the base of an imaginary candle. "It was lit, and the wax had started to melt down. There were a few drops on her hands and her chest, but I don't think it had been burning for long."

Laura nodded. She reached out and put a hand on Waters's shoulder for a moment, a brief reassurance. "Thank you. Was the first body similar? Evelina Collins, right?"

"Right," Waters said. He turned his back on the spot where Ashley Christianson had lain, as if he needed to put it out of his head. "Yes, it was almost identical, I'd say. She was clothed, the same thing with her neck and the blood. She had the candle in her hands the same way. It was earlier in the evening, though. We had that one called in by a local who was walking by the alley and saw her."

Laura checked her watch. It was already ten in the morning. If this pattern held up – a body at night after two days – then they only had until nightfall to make some progress here.

Standing in the street wasn't going to facilitate that.

26

"Let's go to the coroner," she said to Waters as well as to Won. "I need to see these bodies."

CHAPTER SIX

The coroner's office was tiny, a small and low building right next to the precinct, looking like it had been built as an afterthought at a later date. Laura took it in with a sinking feeling, wondering if they were about to walk into something that was far from state of the art. Waters led them inside with a confident stride, only glancing once at the two cops who were standing outside the precinct door watching them. He even put on a little of a swagger. Showing off to his co-workers, Laura thought.

Once inside, the already cool temperature dropped noticeably. Laura had braced for it and didn't react but Won shivered. Through another set of double doors, they walked right into the morgue – with no reception desk or any kind of security, Laura noted. Maybe not a good sign.

"Hey, Tone, you here?" Waters called out. Laura had a moment to glance around the small space: two metal trays which held draped sheets over bodies, with no room for a third. A wall at the far side equipped with metal drawers, the kind for storing more bodies, and a large sink on the right. The left held a small desk and an ancient-looking computer.

A door at the back of the room opened, and an elderly-looking woman with wiry gray hair sticking out around thick glasses appeared. She fixed sharp eyes on them that seemed owlishly large behind the lenses, squinting as she moved forwards.

"No need to yell so loudly, Scott," she said, her voice as sharp as her eyes. Maybe she wasn't as elderly as she'd first appeared – or at least, not as feeble. "I'm right here."

"I've got the FBI agents with me," Waters said, indicating Won and Laura with a thumb jerked over his shoulder. "They want to see the bodies."

Laura glanced at Won at that moment, just in time to notice that his face was extremely pale. She narrowed her eyes.

"Have you done this before?" she asked, hissing it under her breath as Waters and the coroner exchanged a couple of pleasantries.

Won cleared his throat, darting a glance at her before putting his eyes forward again. "No," he admitted. "I mean, yes. Of course. In training. Just not..."

Laura's eyes almost bugged out of her skull. "Have you worked a live murder case before?"

"Well," Won said, which was more than enough to set Laura's blood pressure skyrocketing. "Not, like, *live* exactly. I mean, we did a lot of stuff at the Academy. And I've done some cases since then!"

Laura wanted to ask him what kind of cases, but she looked up to realize that the coroner was now fixing them both with that same sharp glance. Laura had no doubt that the woman had heard and understood everything, even when they were speaking under the cover of her own conversation with Waters.

"Toni Lisle," she said, extending a hand with a quick and birdlike movement. Laura shook it, surprised to find how strong her grip was. "Let's get this show on, then. You'll be wanting to look at them in chronological order?"

Laura nodded once, appreciating the woman's businesslike manner. "That would be ideal, thank you."

Toni nodded sharply back, ambling over to the furthest table. She had that kind of rolling gait that older people often have, a constant compromise between aching muscles and bones. Still, it was clear that her body was the only thing about her that was aged – her mind was functioning as sharply as it ever might have been. She pulled back the sheet with one swift movement, revealing the body of Evelina Collins.

"This, here, is the fatal wound," Toni said, indicating the gaping opening at the neck. "If you'll look closely, you'll see it was a fairly smooth cut. She was not struggling when it happened, and the hand of the killer did not falter."

There was a gagging noise from behind her. Laura turned just in time to see Agent Won running for a trash can and emptying his stomach into it. Given that she knew what exactly was in his stomach – the same stodgy airplane breakfast she'd been subjected to – she couldn't say it was much of a loss. It was disappointing, however. She'd figured he was green as soon as she looked at him. But this... he wasn't just green. He was brand new.

"Get it all out, son," Toni said, the only person in the room to acknowledge it. Waters was looking at the ground, like he didn't want to shame another law enforcement officer. Laura realized she was glaring in Won's direction and took the physical effort required to smooth out her features.

"You can wait outside," she said, trying her hardest to sound sympathetic.

"No," Won said, his voice rough, holding up a hand shakily. "No, I'm good."

"Just make sure you don't go again all over these ladies," Toni said sternly. "Now, as I was saying, it's a smooth cut. Judging by the lack of blood on the skin and the fact we only have lividity on the backs of the bodies, I would say there wasn't a lot of movement just before or after the time of death."

"In other words, they didn't put up a fight," Laura said. She refocused on the task at hand, trying not to keep thinking about the bucket full of Won's sick even though she could smell it now. He would have to handle himself. She'd given him the option to leave, and if he wasn't taking it, that was his choice.

"Didn't, or couldn't," Toni said smartly. She lifted up the arm of the body, letting it sit in the air in front of Laura's face as if she was giving a demonstration. "There's a lack of restraint marks. No marks at all on the rest of the body, in fact. But what I did find is traces of chloroform in the blood."

"He knocks them out, lays them down somewhere, and cuts their throats. Then he carries them away from the blood – maybe washes them, first? And places them in a public spot for someone to find them," Laura translated. Won made a noise in his throat from the foot of the table and retreated back towards the trash can a couple of steps, though this time he managed not to throw up.

"Then adds the candle," Toni said, turning the hand in the other direction. Now Laura could see the back of it, the way it was crusted with dried white wax.

"This is very... gentle," Laura said, though it felt admittedly strange to be saying it in regard to a murder. "They wouldn't have suffered at all. They'd have felt the cloth over the mouths, or... do you think it was a cloth?"

Toni nodded, pointing to a few things around the nose and mouth area that didn't look like anything at all to Laura. "Clear signs of inhalation here and here."

"Alright. They'd have felt something go over their mouths, maybe a brief moment of fear, and then nothing. He kills them without hurting them. Quick and painless. Then he washes them clean, carries them and places them down gently. He finally puts the candle on the chest, almost like a memorial, and then calls someone to come and find them. He doesn't even undress them. There's a kind of respect here."

"Respect?" Waters said, almost scoffing. "He killed them. What kind of respect is that?"

Laura looked up and met his eyes. "Believe me. I've seen a lot of killers. A lot of victims. This... well, it's oddly reverential. It's like a form of worship. Your average killer doesn't take this much care – not even the ones who have their own rituals."

"Maybe it is a ritual," Won croaked. Laura looked up at him with some surprised. He looked a little steadier now, like he was getting a grip back on himself. "He might have some twisted way of doing it. Maybe it's, like, a cult thing."

Laura chose to ignore the mention of the word 'cult.' It was never a cult. That only happened in movies. And the second someone said that word to the press, they would have a field day – which wouldn't be useful to anyone. "If it is a ritual, then it's fairly advanced already," Laura said. "Both women have the same hallmarks?"

Toni nodded. She pulled back the sheet over Ashley Christianson, revealing the same story told in a second body. Laura glanced between the two women quickly. There were similarities, yes – both were young women, after all. One blonde, one brunette. One a little shorter than the other. Ashley's body appeared clean from here, while Evelina had a butterfly tattooed on the side of her stomach.

"Right," Laura said, confirming it with her own eyes. "So, this feels almost like care. Like he's recreating something that he's done before or seen done before. A way of looking after someone. Washing the body – it puts you in mind of a funerary practice, doesn't it? The candle, too."

"I'd say so," Waters nodded. Laura shot a brief smile at him, even though she hadn't actually been asking. She was really just thinking out loud.

"What's the connection between the two of them?" she asked. "Did they both attend your school?"

Waters shook his head. "Evelina was new in town a few years back. As far as we know, there's no obvious connection. They both lived here, probably saw each other around, but that's about all."

"Their jobs?" Laura asked.

"Evelina worked at a coffee shop, and Ashley at a restaurant, right?" Won said, clearly keen to remind them that he was still in the room in order to recover from his earlier weakness.

"Yeah," Waters said, casting him a look of pleased surprise. Laura almost wanted to roll her eyes. She'd read the briefing notes, too. She'd just wanted to check. "So, they didn't work together at all. but like I said, they might have known each other. Just because most folks do, around here."

Laura took a moment to appreciate the fact that she didn't live in a place like Paradise Cove. It was bad enough when everyone at the office knew about your business. Having a whole town always aware of what you were up to, always talking about you, would have been unbearable.

Especially for someone with an ability like Laura's, which was hard enough to hide when she had the excuse of being able to pass it off as investigative talent.

"Alright," Laura said, taking a breath of the cold air inside the morgue and regretting it. It smelled like bleach, the faint scent of entrails, and Won's vomit. "We'd better keep moving. I'd like to talk to the families, next. See if they can shed any light on this." She turned, brushing her hands very deliberately over those of the women on the tables on either side of her: first Evelina, then Ashley. Just in case.

But there was no vision.

At least for now, Laura was on her own. But there was plenty she could manage with that real investigative talent that didn't rely at all on her visions. And she was determined to bring all of it to bear before someone else had to die – especially given it was beginning to feel like she was the only person who wasn't out of her depth on this case.

***

Mr. and Mrs. Collins faced Laura like engravings, both of them sallow and long faced, the signs of grief almost etched into their cheeks. They had obviously been crying for a long time, both of them. Looking at them, Laura figured that by now, on the third day since their daughter's death, they had reached the stage when it feels like the body has no more tears to give.

It did, of course. But the numbness was a special phase itself.

"We just don't understand it," Mrs. Collins said, distantly. She was worrying a handkerchief between her fingers, turning the edges over and over between them. "Why anyone would want to…"

"I'm sure you've spent a lot of time over the last couple of days thinking about this," Laura said gently. "Is there anyone that comes to mind that ever had a problem with your daughter? An ex-boyfriend, a customer, someone from school – anything at all?"

"No," Mrs. Collins said, sniffling slightly. She reached over and took a framed photograph that was sitting beside their sofa, passing it to Laura. It was almost an instinctive gesture, as if she'd passed it to a number of people over the past few days. "No, there wasn't ever anything serious. Look at her. She's so beautiful."

Laura did look, because she could do that much for the grieving mother. Evelina was grinning in the picture, a graduation photograph in her gown. She was about to throw her cap up into the air, by the looks of the shot. She looked happy, carefree. Younger than the body Laura had seen, but yes, pretty. Still, that didn't mean anything about personality – and Laura had cause to know, more than most, that beauty in itself could even be a motive for murder. The killers who had sexual motives went after women who turned them on. Those who were in her shadow could experience dark jealousy, later turning to rage. Beauty was no armor at all.

"You said nothing serious," Laura said, handing the photograph to Won to give him something to do. He was perched beside her in an armchair, doing his best to put on an expression that was both sympathetic and keen, as if to show that he was definitely paying attention. "What about the things that weren't serious?"

Mrs. Collins shrugged, looking at her husband in a kind of helpless gesture.

"Regulars at the café," he said, speaking up for the first time. He had a quiet deference about him, like he preferred for his wife to do the talking. Laura always wondered, in these situations, whether she was seeing the people as they really were – or whether it was grief layered over them in sheets, concealing them, turning them into someone else. "A few of them could be kind of jerks. She complained to us about them sometimes when she came home from her shifts. But nothing that would make us suspicious. Just normal kind of stuff."

Laura nodded. "Did she have a large group of friends?"

"Oh, yes, she settled in here so well, didn't she?" Mrs. Collins said, prompting a mournful nod from Mr. Collins. "She made so many

33

friends. She dated a couple of times, I think, but it never went beyond dates. She was young. She wasn't taking anything too seriously yet."

She pressed the handkerchief against her mouth suddenly, as if she'd just heard what came out of it. Laura's heart went out to her. She was sure that, in Mrs. Collins's position, she would be doing much the same: imagining all of the things her daughter would now never do.

Laura hated thinking like that. It was too real, with Lacey around to pin those fears on. She wrenched her mind back from that brink before she had a chance to topple over it.

"Thank you," Laura said, getting ready to stand up and leave. "Those are all the questions I have for now. We'll leave you in peace – but if we think of anything else, we'll be back."

"Oh, Mrs. Collins," Waters said, moving suddenly from the doorway where he'd been watching them. "I almost forgot. Toni said she doesn't need all of Evelina's things, and the chief approved me bringing her keychain over. They both said there's no evidential value to it and thought you might find some small comfort in having it back."

"Wait a second," Laura said, just as Waters was moving across the room with something in his hands. It wasn't an evidence bag, that was clear. "Let me see that?"

He glanced quickly at the Collins before handing it over with a kind of apologetic gesture, as if to say he really had wanted to give it to them, but Laura had a higher rank. Laura took it, and the first brush of her fingers across it sent a stab of pain into her forehead. An excellent kind of pain. The kind she had been waiting for, to give her a –

Laura was looking at a flame. Right at it. It filled her whole vision, the only thing she could see. Everything was so clear and bright – the yellow-gold tinged with amber around the edges, through to the small core of blue, the hottest part of it. It danced and leapt in some unseen, unfelt wind. It was almost enchanting.

Laura blinked, looking down at the keychain in her hand. There were only a couple of keys on it, evidently house keys. Almost definitely for the very property they were sitting in now. There was a plastic dog attached to it, a stress relieving toy, the novelty kind that made the pug's eyes bulge out when you squeezed it. Laura turned it over in her hands for a moment. Since it wasn't bagged up, there was no point in insisting that it was returned to the lab – any forensic value it had was contaminated already.

But it had given her one very useful thing. A vision. Even though she didn't know what it meant yet, the presence of a flame was no coincidence. It had to have some connection to the killer and his penchant for candles.

All of which meant she was on the right track.

Laura handed the keychain over to Mrs. Collins, seeing no need to keep it from her any longer. Waters was right, it would probably be a comfort for her.

But that didn't stop Laura from taking him aside, just as they were leaving the house, and giving him the clearest warning that she could muster: "Don't release any other items related to the case before speaking to me first. Got that? Every little thing could be evidence."

Waters swallowed and nodded, and she didn't fail to notice how a sympathetic look passed between him and Won a moment later. Two young and inexperienced investigators empathizing with one another on how difficult the job was, when you were up against someone who knew what they were doing.

"Right," Laura said, seeing no reason to dwell on the mistakes. They needed to keep moving forward. It was already past noon, and the killer wasn't going to be waiting for them to get settled in. "Now. Let's go visit Ashley Christianson's family."

CHAPTER SEVEN

Laura took the seat that was offered to her, sitting opposite Diana Christianson. The woman was the kind of formidable matriarch you expected to see in a family drama show: strong, tall, and upright, her makeup intact and her face stony despite the grief she was no doubt feeling.

"Thank you for talking with us," Laura said, hoping to break the ice a little before getting into the questions. "We're doing everything we can to catch the person who did this. With your help, we might get a little closer."

"I spoke to Detective Waters and his colleague yesterday," Diana said, a tremor around her upper lip the only outward sign of the distress that she must have been feeling. "Surely, you already have enough information."

"Sometimes, going over the same ground more than once can help to trigger something," Laura said, trying to keep her smile gentle. "I'm sure Detective Waters and the local police here are more than capable, but now that the case has been escalated to the FBI, we like to hear things for ourselves. Having that outsider perspective can make a real difference."

Diana made a kind of motion with her hand, a move that traveled to her lip as well. A permission to continue, even if she didn't quite seem to agree with the reasoning.

"Are you aware, first of all, of there being any connection between your daughter and Evelina Collins?" Laura asked. She didn't make any attempt to hide the reason why she was asking about the other woman. In a bigger city, you could say a name and not mention why you were bringing it up, and the other party wouldn't know. But here, it was obvious that everyone in town would already know the name of the first victim, whether they'd seen it in the news or just heard it from a neighbor on the street.

"I'm not," Diana said. Then she shook her head, just slightly. "But Ashley is – *was* twenty-two. She has a whole life that I'm not really involved in. I suppose it's possible they could have met at the diner, or even through mutual friends."

36

Laura nodded. So far, so expected. "And how about Ashley herself – do you remember her talking about anyone who might have held a grudge? Someone she fell out with, even a while ago? An ex, things like that?"

"Not really," Diana said. Her fingers twitched slightly, her eyes darting towards an ashtray on the side table by the sofa. It was clean. Laura guessed that Diana had quit smoking some time ago, but now in the hour of her grief, the urge was back. "But there was one customer at the diner. A bit of a stalker."

"A stalker?" Laura said, pricking her ears up. She looked at Detective Waters briefly. He hadn't mentioned this in the briefing notes, nor since meeting them at the town border. He shifted a little, looking uncomfortable, as though he'd been caught out. "Tell me about him."

"He would go into the diner when Ashley was working her shift," Diana said. Her fingers played restlessly on a cushion beside her, as if she wanted nothing more than to be holding a cigarette. "She said it was nothing, but I kept thinking she needed to keep an eye on him. You do read stories."

"What kind of behavior did she report?" Laura asked. "Was it just that he was always going in when she was on shift, or was there more to it?"

"He would leave her notes," Diana said. "Things like a napkin with his number on it. Or a compliment on the bill beside the tip amount. She said he was always watching her, too. Like his eyes would follow her around the room."

"Did you ever witness this yourself?" Laura asked.

Diana nodded, once. "Briefly. I was in there for lunch and saw him talking to her. When I asked her what it was about, since she looked uncomfortable, she told me he'd gone there to ask her out."

"And she turned him down?"

"Yes, apparently quite a number of times. She said it was harmless, but she didn't like having to do it." Diana sighed, "She was a nice girl. Much nicer than I am. I would have told him to buzz off a long time ago and asked the other staff not to serve him. But she said she didn't mind him coming in and being a customer, since all he ever did was ask her out."

"Do you have his name?" Laura asked, flipping open her notebook to take it down.

"Colt Peake," Diana said. "I did mention him to Detective Waters." This last was said with a reproving look at the man himself, who shifted from foot to foot awkwardly where he stood near the door.

Laura glanced at Agent Won. It was a practice born out of habit – normally, she would wait to see if Nate had anything more to ask before wrapping up the conversation. But this time, she was actually glad that Agent Won was keeping his mouth shut. Waters, too. So long as Laura could run this show and not have to field any stupid interruptions from either of them, she would be happy.

"One last thing," she said, because she already felt that Diana was the kind of woman who would have said up-front if she had any other suspicions, rather than keeping them until asked. "Can you think of any significance that a candle would have for Ashley?"

Diana didn't frown at the reference. Clearly, the local PD had already shared the specifics of the crime with her. She only shook her head. "I guess that's something the killer knows more about than I would."

Laura stood up. "Thank you, Ms. Christianson," she said. "I'll leave you my card, in case something else comes to mind."

Diana nodded but didn't get up to show them out. Her fingers twitched again. Laura had the feeling that the moment they were gone, she was going to light up.

Laura led the two junior officers out of the house and back onto the sidewalk outside, into a bright sun that did little to dispel the cold air coming off the sea. Still, Laura reflected again that it was refreshing rather than bracing. There was a stuffiness about being in the home of someone who had suffered a recent loss. Breathing fresh air again felt good.

"Well, this is it, right?" Agent Won said excitedly.

Laura wheeled on him, glaring. She pulled him further away from the house, back towards the two cars parked along the street, before replying. "Don't be so loud. Bear in mind that the relatives of our victim can probably hear you if you start yelling right outside their house."

"Sorry," Won said, though he didn't seem to be completely apologetic. "But we've got him now. We should go arrest him and wrap this all up."

Laura wasn't so convinced. She turned to Detective Waters. "Why didn't you mention this lead to us before?"

"She made it seem like it wasn't a big deal before," Waters said, squirming a little. His hand went up to rub the back of his neck. "And I know Colt. I don't think he would do something like this. He's a little creepy sometimes, sure, but he just doesn't know how to talk to people."

"Hmm." Laura leaned on the side of the car for a moment, thinking. "It would be a big leap. From stalking to murder. And you're not aware of any connection to Evelina?"

"No, ma'am," Waters said. "That's why I didn't think it was important."

"Detective Waters," Laura said, evenly. "You remember how I asked you to defer to me first before giving potential evidence back to the families?"

"Yes," he said. His eyes went a little wider, like he was expecting he was about to get yelled at.

"I'm going to ask you to also defer to me on whether something's important or not," she said. "Did you learn anything else that you haven't disclosed yet?"

Waters hung his head and looked at the floor. His eyes raced back and forth across it, like he was panicking as he searched his memory. "I don't think so."

He looked like he'd been told off by his high school principal. Laura didn't exactly enjoy playing the bad guy, but she was starting to feel like she was looking after a couple of teenagers who didn't know how to play by the rules. Why couldn't Rondelle at least have given her someone with a little more experience, if she was coming to a place where the locals had no experience either? She hated to be a hard ass, but this was an ongoing murder case. There wasn't time to spare anyone's feelings, not when doing so could lead to another death.

"Good." Laura sighed. "We'd better go talk to this Colt Peake, either way. We can't leave any stone unturned if we're going to solve this case."

"Right," Waters said, fumbling to get his car keys out of his pocket. "He lives out by the beach. I'll take you there right now."

"Thank you," Laura said, turning to get into their rental car while Waters walked a few paces ahead to the patrol car.

Inside, Agent Won turned to her with that same enthusiasm that was beginning to grate on her nerves. "This is going to be him," he said. "I can feel it in my bones. We're going to arrest him, and he'll probably fold and confess. I bet he's one of those shy guys who doesn't know how to talk to girls, and then he just snapped. You know, you read about them online. They get really angry about it. Incels."

"We'll see," Laura said, paying more attention to the road as she started the engine and pulled out. "I wouldn't get too excited just yet. Everything's only a lead until we prove it."

"We'll be on the way home before the evening," Agent Won said gleefully, apparently ignoring what she'd said.

Laura sighed, following Detective Waters through the streets of Pacific Cove and wondering which of her particular sins had been the one to make her deserve this.

***

When Laura had heard that Colt Peake lived by the beach, she'd pictured a sunny little apartment, maybe even a beach hut. Something bright and cheerful and, although probably cheap, quite luxurious compared to what the same money might buy in the city.

She couldn't have been further wrong.

Detective Waters led them to an apartment building that looked shabbier than most of the rest of town, far out to the side in an area that didn't seem to be as frequented as other parts. There was a beach, but it was mostly pebbles, unlike the smooth sandy areas that seemed to surround the rest of Pacific Cove. And he led them not to the main entrance of the block, which opened into a sun-filled atrium beyond a modern intercom system, but around the side – to the basement door.

He knocked for them, then seemed to think better of being so forward and stepped behind Laura, causing them all to have to shuffle awkwardly around one another on the stairs down to the basement. He cleared his throat a couple of times as he went, as if in recognition of the fact he'd made it more difficult rather than better.

"Detective Waters," Laura said, at length, as they waited for the knock to be answered. "Why don't you wait by the cars? We don't want to come on too strong."

Of course, what she actually meant was that there were too many cooks hanging around right now. It was enough that she had to deal with Agent Won. Having someone there who knew Colt personally already was only going to complicate matters further, and they didn't need that at all.

The door finally opened as Detective Waters moved away, having nodded at her with a peculiar expression which Laura interpreted as a mixture of shame (at being sent away) and relief. She turned her full attention onto the occupant of the basement as he came into view, hanging onto the door awkwardly like it was a comfort blanket. He was shorter than Laura, shorter than the average man in fact, and a little pudgy. His dark hair was worn messy, like he hadn't bothered to brush or style it, and he was wearing a faded t-shirt bearing some kind of cartoon character.

"Colt Peake?" Laura said, which only made him seem to shrink back behind his door even more.

"Yes," he said, his voice a shadow of a ghost and full of doubt. His skin was pasty pale, like he didn't spend a lot of time in the sun, and scarred with acne pits.

Laura showed him her badge; a movement in the periphery of her vision told her Agent Won had copied her motion. "My name is Special Agent Laura Frost with the FBI. I'd like to ask you a few questions. Can we come inside?"

Colt sniffed, turned, and nodded. He drifted away from the door, leaving it open, which was at least a sort of invitation. Laura stepped inside after him, mentally bracing herself. There was a chance that Colt was the killer, even if she didn't quite believe it.

And even if he wasn't, there was something about a basement apartment that always made her feel a little on edge.

They walked through shadows into a living room that was barely lit. There were windows high up, right at the bottom of street level, thin and narrow, but these had short blinds pulled over them anyway. The only light was the screen of a television, turned on but not in use, showing only the landing screen of a popular games console. It took up most of one wall, with the rest of the furniture consisting only of a battered old leather sofa, a coffee table littered with takeout containers and empty cans of energy drinks, and a stack of games that towered up next to the television.

Colt sat down heavily on his own sofa as Laura and Agent Won followed him, causing a stray chip to temporarily raise up into the air at the breeze of his passing. He hugged his arms tight across his chest as he sat, and then moved hastily to cover something that was sitting on the arm of the sofa – though Laura saw it before he had a chance to.

"Is that a photograph of Ashley Christianson?" she asked, almost incredulous. Surely, a killer wouldn't leave such an obvious clue laying around and then draw even more attention to it by trying to cover it in a

41

hurry. Not one who had the ability to drop a body in the middle of a public place without being seen.

"N-no," Colt said, pressing his arm deeper onto the cushion he had placed on top of it, as if that was going to help him at all.

Laura simply held out her hand.

Colt swallowed, then pulled the photograph out from under the cushion and handed it to her. It was framed, but it was far from a professional photograph. It was a little blurry, showing Ashley in a plain waitress uniform of a black shirt and pants with a red apron around her waist. She was smiling at someone else, probably leaning over to take an order judging by the pad and pen in her hands. It was clear it had been taken unawares, probably by Colt sitting on the other side of the room with his phone.

"No?" Laura prompted, just to make Colt talk.

"I... I just heard about it yesterday," Colt said, his voice sounding wretched. "I can't believe it still. It's... I can't believe that she's really gone."

"Can't you?" Agent Won said, speaking up. Laura felt a sinking feeling in her chest at his words. Oh, no. He was going to mess this up, wasn't he? "I find that strange, considering that you are the person who took her life."

Colt stared at him with his eyes so wide, it was like some unseen force was pulling them open behind his control. His already pale face paled even further, his lips quivered, and Laura realized only then that there were already tear tracks on his face. They glistened slightly in the green-tinted light from the television when he dared to turn his head.

Won had done it, now. Laura stayed silent. Better to let the suspect react than try to take control back. Maybe he would do something incriminating.

"N-no," he said, shaking his head slowly. "No, I'm not."

Or not.

Laura shot a warning glance at Agent Won to stay silent before continuing. "Why do you have this photograph, Colt? It doesn't look as though Ashley knew she was being photographed here."

"I just... I wanted to look at her," Colt said, the words tumbling out of his mouth as though he was in no control at all. "I wanted to be able to see her all the time, even when I wasn't at the diner. I couldn't afford to eat there all the time."

"But why take a photograph without her knowledge?" Laura pressed. "You could have asked her to pose with you."

42

Colt's face worked, his lips trying to form something before his tongue caught up. "I did ask her."

"She said no." Laura tilted her head as she looked at him, giving him a steely glare. "But you took one anyway."

"I didn't..." Colt was like a man made of jelly, his whole body quivering, his lips wobbling even more than the rest. "I didn't think it would do any harm. I just wanted to see her face all the time! She's so beautiful – was so beautiful – I just..."

He was practically falling to pieces in front of them. Laura had no doubt at all that he was innocent of murder. He might have been guilty of stalking behavior, and he was definitely a bit of a creep, but that was all. There was no way he had the strength and mental acuity to pull off this kind of attack, lay a body out in public, and then calmly call the police to tell them where to find it.

Laura had seen killers who faked it before. Even on her last case, she'd come up against a paramedic who seemed totally charming and friendly on the surface, only to later realize she'd been talking to a killer all along. But this kid? He was scared, and grieving. He'd clearly been in love with Ashley – infatuated, even. But he was weak. And not the kind of weak that led people to kill. The kind that led them to cower in basements and never do anything to change their lives.

If he had been a killer, Laura could see that it would have been sexually motivated. That was the kind of murder someone like Colt Peake would commit – he wouldn't be able to resist getting his grubby little hands on Ashley, either before or after killing her. There didn't seem to be that kind of angle to this case, and Colt had no connection to Evelina anyway.

They were wasting their time here, just like Detective Waters had thought.

"Did she say no to you one too many times?" Agent Won asked. "Is that why you killed her? Because if you couldn't have her, you didn't want anyone else to either?"

"What?" Colt said, looking at Laura as if expecting her to save him. "No!"

"What about Evelina Collins? Did she turn you down, too?"

Colt frowned, which on top of his still shocked and scared open mouth and eyes made him look like a Halloween mask. "No! I didn't – I wouldn't...!"

"You're going to have to do better than that," Won said, grabbing a pair of handcuffs that he'd had stuffed in his belt. "You're going to

43

have to explain this at the precinct. Colt Peake, I'm arresting you on suspicion of murder."

And Colt Peake looked at him like he was about to burst into tears and wet himself at the same time.

CHAPTER EIGHT

"Woah!" Laura exclaimed, holding up a hand and staring at Agent Won. "Agent Won – a word."

She pulled at Agent Won's arm when he tried to step past her anyway, obviously intent on delivering the handcuffs that he had pulled out. He looked at her with a half-pleading expression, putting her in mind of nothing more than a little boy whose mother was telling him off in front of his friends. But he gave way, stumbling around and turning back towards the exit when she pushed him.

He'd gone too far. She was supposed to be the senior agent here, and they hadn't discussed this. Besides the fact that she was sure he was wrong, he was also coming on way too strong – like an FBI agent from a movie, not someone who had to deal with real-life people.

This was a basement apartment – only one way in and out. They weren't risking an escape attempt by leaving Colt Peake on his own. Not that Laura believed for even a moment he was really the person they needed to be arresting, anyway.

Laura didn't stop moving, or pushing Agent Won along in front of her, until they got outside of the apartment again and were standing at the bottom of the stairs.

"What are you doing?" Laura hissed immediately.

"What am I doing?" Agent Won replied, giving her a boggle-eyed look. "What are *you* doing? Why did you stop me? We need to take him in!"

"No, we really don't," Laura said. She folded her arms across her chest. "Have you forgotten that I'm the senior agent on this case? You're supposed to run things like this past me before you take any action!"

"Is that it?" Agent Won said, groaning. "Sorry. I got excited. I could see he needed taking in, so I just wanted to be the one to do it."

"No, that's not it," Laura snapped, shaking her head at him. "We don't need to take him in. He doesn't have anything to do with this murder."

"What?" Agent Won gaped, then gestured behind her, towards the apartment. "Didn't you hear him? He was stalking her! He took that picture without her permission and then he tried to hide it from us – and her mother already told us to watch out for him. It's got to be him!"

"That's a mighty big assumption to make from very few facts," Laura warned him. "Don't forget, Agent Won, that the choices we make here affect people's lives. What do you think happens when we drag in somebody for questioning?"

Agent Won stared at her like he wasn't sure the answer would be so obvious, and yet it was obvious to him. "We get to question them?"

"No," Laura said. "We can question them whenever we want. Right here at home, for example. But when we take them in, people see it. The press get wind of it. Names and reputations get dragged through the mud, and sometimes they don't recover."

"So we're supposed to just let him get away with it or something?" Agent Won scoffed. "I did the training. I know if we interrogate him at the precinct in front of a camera and tapes, we can use it in court. Otherwise, it would just be our testimony against his."

"No, we're supposed to be sure," Laura said. "A lot more sure than we are right now. We've barely even spoken to the guy. Did you think about asking him for an alibi?"

Agent Won opened his mouth, then closed it again. "I thought we would do that at the precinct," he said, eventually.

"How about doing it right now?" Laura said. She shook her head. "You haven't been doing this long enough to have a gut instinct yet. You need to look at facts and evidence before you do anything rash. And don't go jumping the gun."

"I'm good at this," Agent Won insisted. "I scored really high at the Academy. And I'm good at reading people. Just because I haven't done as many cases as you, you can't just assume I'm wrong all the time!"

"I'm not assuming," Laura said. "I'm using my own skills. Let's go inside, shall we, and hear what he has to say for himself?"

Agent Won's nostrils flared for a moment before he let out a heavy breath. "You undermined me in front of him," he said.

"You undermined me by acting without my approval," Laura corrected him. "Do it again, and I'll do the same thing. You're a rookie. I'm the senior agent. That's the way it has to be."

"I'm not just a rookie," he said, petulantly, before pushing past her and back into the apartment.

Laura let that go with a sigh. She turned to go into the apartment after one last look at the sky above them, a much brighter-seeming sight in comparison to the dingy basement. It was getting on into the later part of the afternoon, and this was a waste of time.

She let her hand touch the wall as she moved along the corridor back to the living room, guiding her own steps. Her hand landed on fabric instead: a scrap of red she hadn't noticed hanging on the wall before. A flare of pain hit her head, and before she had a chance to think about why –

The flames were dancing again, just like in her last vision. Floating in front of her eyes, bending to an invisible current, making shapes that seemed to torment her until she saw things that weren't there. And then – a darkness. The flames, snuffed out. Just the light impression of smoke bending away into the darkness. Like a candle being blown out.

Laura blinked, clearing her head. She took the scrap of fabric with her as she moved back to join Colt and Agent Won, examining it more closely. It looked familiar. Very familiar.

"What is this?" she asked, coming to a stop in front of Colt, right next to Agent Won. For his part, Won was silent, almost sulky, like he didn't want to speak until he was given permission now. Good.

Colt wet his lips. "It's a bit of her apron," he said. "I... I didn't do anything! It was an old one and it ripped, and she threw it in the trash! I just... saw, and... I saved it. That's all!"

Laura sighed. This boy was in need of a lesson in not going too far, but that was all. She had to end this, leave before Agent Won jumped to another conclusion. "Where were you on Saturday night?"

"I was at the Fresh Catch," Colt said.

"The Fresh Catch?"

"The diner where Ashley worked," Agent Won supplied, looking a surly kind of smug that he'd known something she hadn't.

"And after she finished her shift?" Laura prompted.

"I stayed there late," Colt said. "I... I paid for the food, so I wanted to stay at the table for as long as possible. I didn't want to come home. She told me she wasn't going to go out with me again, and I... I was feeling down. I was there until closing. You can ask anyone else who works there!"

"Alright," Laura said, deciding this whole thing was done. For a moment she thought about throwing the apron scrap over to Colt, but it was better that he didn't have it. It had triggered one vision already, and besides, she didn't want him to think his behavior was fine. "I'm keeping this. Get a new hobby. And for God's sake, when a girl tells

47

you she's not interested, *move on.* You're lucky no one has filed charges against you yet."

Laura turned, ignoring the flabbergasted look on Colt's face. He'd just experienced what was probably the equivalent of a bombshell for him. Thinking he would be arrested, then not being, then being dealt a harsh truth. He was going to have to deal with that on his own. Or with the local police, whichever came first.

She'd known already she was right about him being innocent. Now she was even more sure, and the vision had solidified it.

There was importance in those flames. She had seen them twice, now. She was getting the feeling that they weren't just something the killer set up on the body. They were more than that. Maybe something intrinsically connected to him, like through his job or something. Some aspect of his personality that would lead them right to him.

Laura stepped outside into the fresh air gratefully, checking her cell phone as they walked back to the car. No new messages. She'd been hoping for something from Rondelle, maybe. She bit her lip slightly, watching Agent Won stalk back to the car like a teenager in the middle of a petulant fit.

If she didn't sort out this thing with Nate, she was going to be stuck with Agent Won instead. She didn't want that. She'd rather work alone.

"Get in the car and wait for me," Laura said, almost hating the way it came out sounding like an order. But only almost, because it *was* an order. She apparently had to tell him every little thing, or he was going to go off the rails and arrest every passerby and his dog. It was too much like babysitting. She hated it.

Up ahead of them, Detective Waters was leaning by his own car, looking awkward and trying to pretend he couldn't read Agent Won's body language. It must have been fairly obvious that they'd had an argument. Laura gestured to him wordlessly from where she stood rather than moving closer to talk, indicating that she was going to make a call and then go. He got into his car, taking the hint to not eavesdrop on her call.

She dialed for Rondelle, knowing he was probably going to be annoyed with her for calling in the middle of a case but unable to help herself.

"Division Chief Rondelle speaking."

"Hi, Chief," Laura said. "Look, I was thinking about this whole transfer thing."

Rondelle sighed. "I know he's a bit eager, but that's what they're like fresh out of the Academy. I know you don't remember it, but you were like that once as well. Just give him a chance."

"It's not that," Laura said. Although it very much was that. "It's about Nate. I was thinking, can't you delay his transfer? Maybe long enough that he has to come back to work to avoid using up all his annual leave? He's avoiding my calls, but if I can just speak to him..."

"Laura," Rondelle said, with the kind of fatherly admonishment that only a paternal figure could muster. Which he was, really – for everyone in his division. "You know I can't do that. My hands are tied. I've already put the paperwork in. As soon as it clears, he'll be moving on."

"Well, what if the paperwork got pulled back?" Laura said. "Maybe you filled in something wrong on the form and you realized, and you want to correct it before filing it again."

Rondelle made a noise in his throat, and she could imagine him shaking his head with that sharp look in his eyes. "I'm going to pretend you didn't just suggest that I tamper with employee paperwork in order to suit your own personal agenda," he said. "Aren't you supposed to be catching a murderer right now?"

"Yes, sir," Laura sighed. At least she'd tried.

Rondelle ended the call first, clearly not in the mood to hear any more of her complaints. Laura sighed and got into the car, resting her hands on the steering wheel for a moment as she contemplated their next move.

"We should at least check his alibi," Agent Won said. He seemed to be subtly fuming under the surface. He was still hung up on it, apparently.

"We can ask Detective Waters to do that," Laura said. "It's not a priority, and we need to delegate. I've got a better idea."

"What?" Agent Won asked, in a tone that implied he didn't really think there was any other possibility that could be better than the lead he'd come up with personally.

"The candles," Laura said. She trusted in her vision. She was seeing flames for a reason. "We need to go back and look at them. Find out who made them, where they might have been purchased from. This is a small town, and the killer is probably a local. If we're lucky, it's going to be some kind of niche handcrafted product that only exists here for the tourists, and they're going to have credit card records leading us to someone who just bought a bunch of them, and we'll be able to bring in a new suspect."

"Oh," Agent Won said, looking somewhat abashed. He turned to face the front windscreen. He clearly had no way to argue with this idea and hated it.

"Yes, oh," Laura said. "Evidence and proof, Agent Won." She started the car's engine, well aware that it was extremely hypocritical for an agent who relied on psychic visions to say this to a rookie – but also well aware that there was no way he would ever know she got her leads   from   different   sources.

CHAPTER NINE

He filed into the line behind another man, joining the slow shuffle forward as they all took one step closer to having their turn at the counter. He had a small number of items clutched in his hands: some gum, a candy bar, a music magazine. He didn't really need any of them.

What he did need was an excuse to stand in this line. Her line.

He liked observing her. Sometimes from a little farther away. Sometimes as a customer of hers, when he dared, just like this. Never too much. It would be suspicious if he was here too much. But every now and then, it was a good chance to get really close to her. To hear her speak. To watch her without needing to squint.

Close physically, anyway. They had never been close in another way. Not like that. He'd been watching her for so long, and he'd never been able to get close enough even for a real conversation.

The line shifted up by another customer. Just the guy in front next, and then it would be his turn. He enjoyed the moment, taking her in, making sure not to do it in such a way that she would catch him.

By the counter there were a number of items on sale. A bundle of tea candles caught his eye, and he almost wanted to smile. Their lights were small and went out quickly, which was never going to be right for him. He needed a big statement, a candle that would burn properly, that would take time.

If they burned down too quickly, no one would ever see their light. No one but him, and her. No, for her, he was going to pick out something a lot more special than a discount gas station tealight.

He wanted other people to see it. The light that burned above her when she was laid out for her final rest. It would be a special moment. That was why he had to leave her somewhere public – to make sure that she was found and seen. He couldn't just let her disappear into the darkness and have no one notice it. That wouldn't be right. Not for someone like her.

Last time, he'd been so nervous about Ashley not being found that he'd even called the police himself. Well, not as himself, obviously. He'd used a pay phone that wasn't covered by cameras, and he'd changed his voice a little, and tried not to say anything that would give

51

him away. Just a simple statement, that there was a body and where it was, and that they needed to come look at it. That was all the information they needed. No need to push things by saying more. He'd just wanted to be sure that they would find her.

Ashley had been lovely, and he was glad that he had chosen her. But now that it was done, he had to move on to his next choice. To this woman, even now serving the man in front of him. She had such a lovely voice, even if she didn't use it often enough. Or nicely enough. She could be surly. But he understood that. Working a job like this, you had to deal with a lot of people who weren't worth dealing with. That could be hard.

He didn't blame her for being short with any of them. Even with him. It didn't matter.

Soon they would be closer, close enough to satisfy him. It didn't need to be right now.

The man in front moved away, and it was like a bright spotlight shone down on him, lighting up the way; it was his turn now to be served. To be close to her, just for a moment.

There had been many moments like this in all the time he'd watched her. But soon, these kinds of moments would be over.

Soon, they would be closer than they had ever been – and he couldn't wait.

CHAPTER TEN

Laura glanced up at the darkening sky with unease. It was early evening already, and she had hoped they would be further along than this by now. That there would have been an obvious lead the police had missed, something they could jump on right away. No such luck.

Which was why it was more important than anything that they get this done quickly and get the answers they were looking for.

"Is this it?" Laura asked, checking the GPS again. Without Waters leading them, now that he was back at the precinct, the GPS was their only resource to be sure of whether they were in the right place. The building in front of them appeared to be unmarked. It was just a warehouse of some kind, not looking at all like what she had expected.

Then again, she didn't know what she'd expected. She hadn't ever been to visit a candle factory before.

"Looks like it," Agent Won said. He'd begrudgingly let some of his surliness go when Laura's hunch had turned out to give them something: the name of the manufacturer who produced both of the candles, despite them being slightly different models.

"Alright," Laura shrugged, cutting the engine and opening her door. "Let's get in there fast. It looks like shift changeover time." She nodded towards the rest of the parking lot as she moved; it was full of cars, some of them entering and some of them leaving. People were also streaming in and out of the doors, which complicated matters as she and Won joined the stream to fight through them instead of being just carried along.

Most of the workers knew exactly where they were going, but Laura was able to pull to the side towards a reception desk in the entrance. The building was similarly sparse on the inside: a simple logo, the name of the company in a sensible font, was placed above the desk on a glass plaque, but there was very little other decoration. Everyone seemed to be coming and going from a swinging door on the left, through which Laura glimpsed what appeared to be a staff locker room.

"How can I help you?" the receptionist asked, a wide-eyed look in her eyes that suggested to Laura unexpected visitors here were few and far between.

Laura placed her badge on the desk. "I'm hoping to speak to someone who'd know all the employees here – maybe a supervisor or a manager," she said.

The second she saw the badge, the receptionist seemed to dive into her phone with a kind of rabbit-like terror. "Of course!" she exclaimed. "I'll just call someone through now."

Laura turned her back to the desk for a moment, watching the people coming and going. They seemed not to be one continuous stream of leavers, as she'd thought, but rather dribs and drabs. They left in pairs or alone, occasionally in a slightly larger group, while the employees going into the factory floor appeared to have dwindled to almost nothing. She figured people were taking their time in getting ready, or maybe that they were finishing off specific tasks before setting off for home.

"He'll be out in just a moment," the receptionist said, popping her head back up above the desk.

"Great," Laura said. "What do you guys make here? I mean, candles, obviously, but…"

"Oh, we manufacture a number of different local and national brands," the receptionist said, a gleam in her eyes to be back on familiar ground that she was confident enough to talk about. "There's a number of brand names that you may have heard off." She slid a laminated leaflet across the top of the desk towards her, letting Laura study it. She noticed the brand that was responsible for the candles their killer was using.

"Are there any which are sold only in the local area?" Laura asked.

"Not really," the receptionist said, making a face as if she was disappointed that she couldn't say yes. "We usually send them out to a number of different retailers."

Laura filed that piece of information away. They could be bought in places outside of Pacific Cove. That only made it more likely, in her mind, that the factory being here was not a coincidence. And who would have better access to the products made in the factory – and more of a deeper connection to them – than someone who actually worked here?

"Hello?" said a voice from behind them, and Laura turned at the same time as Agent Won to see a bearded man in a long white coat and cap approaching them. He was overweight but stout, in that way some men have after middle age when they work on their feet all day long. "I'm the floor manager. Justin. I think you wanted to speak to me?"

Laura stepped forward and held out a hand for him to shake. "Justin. I'm Special Agent Laura Frost, and this is Special Agent Eric Won. Is there a private space where we can go to ask you a few questions?"

A troubled look passed over Justin's face, but he nodded and led them in the opposite direction to where the workers were still slowly trickling out of the locker room. The door on the other side of the room took them into what was obviously a meeting space, complete with a meeting table and a long glass panel allowing them to see into the factory itself.

Good for observing the workers. Not good for doing it without being seen themselves.

"We're looking for anyone who might have been exhibiting strange behavior among your employees," Laura said, the moment the door was closed behind them. "For example, maybe someone was caught stealing candles and taking them home?"

Justin glanced behind himself, through the glass panel. "Candles? No." He shrugged his shoulders. "It's not like they're worth a lot of money."

"Have any gone missing recently?" Agent Won asked. He was apparently getting his stride back. Laura let it go this time, given that the question was a sensible one.

Justin shrugged again, scratching the back of his neck. "It's hard to say," he said. "We have a certain amount of waste product – candles that don't quite get made the right shape or where one of the lines malfunctions and we have to throw things away. It would be pretty easy for someone to take a candle here and there without anyone ever noticing it."

Laura nodded, though internally she wanted to scream. Of course. It wouldn't be easy for them, would it? "How about any other kinds of odd behavior? Anyone missing shifts, acting strange compared to what you'd normally expect of them, or so on?"

Justin turned and searched the factory floor, as if he was waiting for someone to trigger his memory. "I don't think so," he said, slowly. "Man, it's hard to think when you ask me on the spot like this."

Laura tried very hard not to lose her patience. He was probably right. If nothing came to mind immediately, perhaps a disciplinary

55

procedure he'd had to carry out recently, then there was likely nothing that stood out enough to be a red flag.

"I'm getting a call," Agent Won said hurriedly, his voice low. "It's Detective Waters."

Laura nodded. "Take it outside," she told him, watching him go with slightly envious eyes. She was sure Detective Waters, who had been tasked with running background checks on the employees at the plant, was going to have something important to say. But he'd called Won, so she would have to wrap up this pointless interview.

Boys would be boys, she supposed. Of course, Waters would call the other young, inexperienced male assigned to the case instead of the scary woman who was both of their superiors. She hated to think of someone characterizing her that way, but she wasn't here to make friends. She was here to solve a case. If he wasn't mature enough to get up the courage to call her directly, then that was his issue.

"How has the reaction been to the recent murders in town?" she asked, thinking that this could be another source of suspicion. "Anyone had a strong reaction to it? Really interested in hearing the latest news, or grief-stricken when you wouldn't expect it, that sort of thing? Or the other way – totally not seeming to care?"

Justin shook his head. "Everyone's been pretty shook up about it," he said. "Those two young girls – it doesn't bear thinking about. Their whole lives ahead of them. And just about everyone here's eaten at the Fresh Catch or had a coffee at Rise and Shine at some point. We knew these girls."

Laura fought for control over her patience again. There had to be *something*. But she couldn't just scream at the man to bring her a result. That wasn't going to make him any more observant. And it was entirely possible that the killer, whoever they were, was doing a good enough job of assimilating that no one had noticed anything.

"Do you know of anyone ever having a problem with either of them?" she asked, just in case, though she was losing hope.

"I'm sorry," he shrugged. "No one. We're a good community here. Everyone gets along for the most part. I wouldn't imagine anyone had any problem with them outside of the odd customer complaint about food."

Laura nodded, pursing her lips together with dissatisfaction. She was going to have to move on. It was a shame, but this man couldn't give her anything.

Maybe it would be worth a chat with the receptionist on the way out, just to tick off a box. Sometimes, people in those kinds of roles would know things that the management didn't.

"Hey!" Agent Won called out, tumbling back into the room breathlessly as if he'd just run back in from outside. "Detective Waters found a match in the system. There's an employee here with a record."

Laura turned wide eyes on Justin. "You didn't think to mention this?"

"What?" he asked, shaking his head. "I don't... who?"

"His name is Toby Martins," Agent Won said. "He has a history of harassment, drug use, and even assault – a couple of arrests in the local area, too. He's been at it for years. And he's a local at the diner, apparently."

A deep frown came across Justin's forehead. "This is the first I'm hearing about this," he said. "Toby didn't declare any criminal record on his application."

"You didn't do a background check?" Laura asked.

"Well," Justin said. A look of slight panic was coming over his face. "I mean, I'm not the *only* person responsible for hiring, and..."

"Never mind," Laura snapped, cutting him off. "You can reassess your company policies later. Where is he? Is he on shift now?"

"Uh," Justin said, glancing towards the factory floor again. "I think his shift just ended. He would have just punched out."

Laura swore. "Come with us, right now!"

She rushed out into the reception area again with Agent Won at her side and Justin only just behind them. She ushered Justin ahead, directing him towards the punch clock she had glimpsed inside the locker room. It was a newer electronic system and, beside it, all the timecards were set up along the wall.

Justin moved with dexterity to the right card, grabbing it out and reading the printed numbers on it. He checked his watch right afterwards. "Seven sixteen," he read. "This was less than two minutes ago. He's probably still in the parking lot!"

That was all Laura needed to hear.

"Car make and model?" she shouted over her shoulder, already springing towards the door.

"I don't know exactly – it's a brown truck with a dented bumper," Justin called back, his voice disappearing as she built up to full speed through the reception area and out into the lot.

There were still plenty of cars out there. Still people moving towards them and driving away, although the influx of arriving employees had stopped. The lateness of the leaving shift meant that many of the spots closer to the door were now empty, with the new arrivals not having been able to park in them. There was a brown truck, right up ahead of them, towards the back of the empty area – like he'd been one of the last to arrive for the last shift.

And there was a man walking right up to the door with his keys held out in his hand.

"Hey!" Laura yelled, still rushing towards him. "Toby Martins!"

He glanced at her, confirming her suspicions that he was indeed the man they were after. He was balding, probably in his fifties, a little overweight. A little greasy. His face was round and white in the gathering gloom, catching the streetlights above the lot. He stared at her for a split second, and in that moment, she saw two things: one, that he understood well enough they were law enforcement, and two, he wasn't going to hang around to see what they wanted.

He cleared the last of the distance to his truck, unlocked it, and jumped into the driver's seat without bothering with a seatbelt.

He was going to try to get away.

Laura gritted her teeth and put on another burst of speed, but she could already see that it was too late. "Stop! FBI!" she shouted, even though she knew realistically that that almost never worked. Actually, it seemed like people were more likely to run from her whenever she told them who she was. But then that was probably because she had a knack for yelling it at people who were actually guilty.

The engine of the truck started. Laura knew this wasn't going to work. She wasn't some kind of athlete, even if she kept in shape enough for the average chase. She wasn't going to be able to chase down a truck. She peeled off to the side, making for where they had parked their rental car, expecting Agent Won to follow.

When she glanced over her shoulder a moment later, he was still heading right for the truck.

Laura swore in her head again, with no breath to actually utter it out loud. She reached the car and fumbled for the door, wrenching it open and throwing herself inside. The truck was squealing out of the parking lot already, and a glance in her rearview mirror as she started the engine and threw the car into reverse showed her Agent Won just narrowly avoiding getting hit by it.

Laura had no time even to shake her head – she had to go. She roared backwards, throwing the car back into drive to speed after him, taking the shortest possible route to the parking lot exit instead of following in the burned rubber he'd already laid down. Agent Won appeared to be trying to give chase on foot, so she ignored him. She had to. There was no time to stop and let him get into the car. He'd already made his choice.

Laura made it to the exit only a few moments after the truck did, but he was moving fast on the road already, putting his foot all the way down and disregarding any street signs or limits. Laura turned onto the road after him and put her own foot to the floor, gripping the steering wheel tightly. She couldn't be afraid to go fast now. She was going to have to catch him, and that meant keeping up with the turns he took, staying on his tail for as long as she had to before he was in cuffs.

Past the parking lot and the factory, they quickly descended into a less populated area. It was only a small town, after all, and the factory was on the outskirts – no doubt planned that way to avoid an eyesore that might put off the tourists. The streetlights petered out, plunging Laura into darkness with only her own headlights and those of the truck to show her the way. She focused on keeping him ahead, taking turn after turn just as he did, not letting him pull away from her.

It was tight. He didn't bother with normal road safety, turning at the last minute every time, forcing her to also wrench the steering wheel hard and shoot after him down increasingly small rural roads, out away from the town now. She had no idea where she was. In the darkness, things loomed up out of nowhere – fence posts alongside the road, large boulders probably set there as markers, hedges, a barrier that told her they were most likely back alongside the sea. She glanced at her GPS to confirm it, and –

He was gone. Where had he gone?!

Laura glanced around in a panic, looking for the telltale sign of headlights, but she could see none. She checked all of her mirrors, slowing down, looking through her windows desperately. Nothing. He must have taken a quick turn and she'd lost him while she was looking away, concentrating on the screen.

Laura swore vehemently for what felt like the fifteenth time and grabbed for her phone, feeling a shot of pain right across her head even before she'd managed to fully rationalize that she needed to call Waters and get an APB –

Flashing lights. Blinking from one side to the other of a sign. A warning. Laura's vision expanded from that one spot of darkness, and she saw more: the barriers down over the crossing, stopping anyone from just driving on through. Tracks. Railroad tracks. There was a train coming.

And there was a brown truck parked in front of the flashing lights.

Laura blinked, realizing she was looking at her phone again. She braked hard, checking the GPS: there was a railroad track across the left side of the map, opposite to the direction of the water, and she'd just passed a turning that appeared to go all the way towards it.

She hit reverse again, zooming back to the trail – little more than a bumpy passage between two fields, with high hedges on both sides obscuring her sight and almost making the turnoff invisible – and took it, powering ahead once more.

There was still no time to lose. The train would go through the crossing; the barriers would open. She had to get to him before that, and she still couldn't see –

She took a slight bend in the track, and up ahead she saw them. Blinking lights. The crossing.

Laura gunned it until she was right on the truck, seeing the driver's side door open in the beam of her headlights. He knew she was on him. He stumbled out and almost fell, dragging himself back to his feet and trying to run, trying to make it across the field. But he was overweight, unfit. Laura was quicker.

She leapt out of her car, drawing her gun the moment she hit the ground and pointing it at his shambling figure. "Freeze, or I'll shoot!" she warned, grabbing her torch with the other hand in case he didn't stop, in case she needed to chase him across the dark fields.

He stopped.

He turned, bringing his hands up above his head, looking at her with an expression she'd seen many times. The fear, regret, and panic of being caught and knowing there was no longer any way out.

She had him now.

She pulled her handcuffs out of her belt, stepping towards him with the gun still held steady just in case he got any more ideas. This time, when she reached for her cell phone, it was going to be to call it in – and get Agent Won to prepare at the precinct to bring Martins in.

CHAPTER ELEVEN

Laura stared through the window of the interview room, watching Toby Martins. The man was sitting there stony-faced and silent, his arms clasped in front of him where the cuffs didn't allow him to fold them over his chest, staring into nothing. He couldn't see Laura through the double-sided glass.

"What are we waiting for?" Agent Won asked. He had been tapping his finger on the table beside the window for at least five minutes, as if Laura didn't know already that he was feeling impatient.

"I told you," she said. "There's no point barging in there and trying to get him to talk all over again. We have to play this carefully and trick him into talking."

"Why can't we just do that now?" Agent Won complained. "I learned this technique in the Academy, where you -"

"Trust me, Agent Won," Laura said through gritted teeth. "They haven't invented any new techniques since I was at the Academy myself. Whatever they taught you, I know it too."

Agent Won slumped a little, then dropped down into the seat by the window. There was only the basics of investigation at the little precinct: a single interview room, with a single control room beside it, where another officer could watch through the window and monitor the recording equipment. It was a little cramped, to say the least.

Laura stayed standing, watching Martins. He hadn't shown much sign of discomfort since they'd brought him in. It was as though none of this was touching him – but through observation, Laura was starting to notice small signs that that wasn't quite the case. When he did reach for the plastic cup of water they'd provided for him – which was not often – his hands were shaking slightly. He took quick, sharp sips, as if afraid to show any vulnerability in his thirst.

"When are we going to go back in there?" Agent Won asked. "If we're waiting, then fine. But when do we stop?"

Laura sighed, turning to face him. *When I say so* was the tempting answer that wanted to roll off her tongue. But even though she didn't much feel like being anyone's mentor, she could at least explain to

Won what she was doing and why. Then he would stop asking her every five minutes, and she could get some peace, at least for the day.

She didn't want to think about the fact that they might remain partnered up for longer, but if they did, she definitely wanted him on the same page as her with this kind of thing.

"What's the one thing he's said over and over again since we brought him in?" Laura asked.

"No comment," Agent Won readily supplied.

"When we asked him why he ran?"

"No comment."

"When we asked him if he wanted a lawyer?"

"No comment."

"When we asked him to confirm his own name?"

"No comment."

"Right." Laura looked at Agent Won evenly. "If you go back in there and try to talk to him again without changing anything, what do you think he's going to say?"

Agent Won looked annoyed to have to say it, but he did: "No comment."

"That's not going to get us anywhere," Laura said, turning back to the window. "I'm not just standing here staring at him, you know. I'm watching. Assessing his mental state."

"What are you looking for?" Agent Won asked.

"Signs that he's beginning to crumble," Laura said. "Look at him right now. He's solid, at least on the outside. On the inside, all kinds of things are going through his head. He's wondering if we have any evidence. Trying to tell himself that we don't. Wondering how long he's been here, how long we're going to keep him. Maybe thinking about getting home, the things he was supposed to be doing tonight. Making dinner. And then he'll go back around – how long am I going to be here for? And all these worries are going to circle around and around in his head until it starts to break him, because there's nothing there to distract him from them."

"What if it doesn't?" Agent Won asked.

"It will," Laura said. She nodded to the window again just as Martins reached out for another jerky, quick sip of his drink. "Look. He's already so nervous he's practically afraid to move. And if it doesn't, well, there's always the backup plan."

"What's the backup plan?"

Laura almost smiled at how easily Agent Won fell into her 'trap' and asked the right question. "The locals," she said. "We asked Detective Waters to go and raid his place, right? The warrant came through, and they'll be there by now. All we have to do is wait. If there's something of evidential value there, we'll have it soon enough. And we can take that into the room to batter down his defenses instead."

"What if that doesn't work?" Agent Won asked.

"Then we try another technique," Laura said. "But believe me, of all the things you learned in your training, the most important is this: people like to fill silences. Right now, he's filling that silence with a dialogue inside his own head, trying to convince himself to stay calm but getting worse and worse at doing so. And once we go in there, he'll already be so nervous that when we leave more silences in the conversation, he'll fill them with stupid things. Things he shouldn't say. That's how we'll get him."

Agent Won said nothing to that, apparently contemplating it in the privacy of his own mind. Laura resumed her own silent vigil, concentrating on Martins. Of course, there were two edges to every sword, and she was doing a pretty good job of filling her own silence with her own thoughts.

Like the statistics that were bugging her: that most killers who took more than one victim in a ritualistic or specific manner like this tended to be on the younger side, before the age of thirty. But Toby Martins was in his fifties. There was also the fact that he didn't look very fit or healthy, yet the person they were looking for had carried the body of an adult and laid it down and then gotten away quickly enough that no one saw them do it.

None of which meant he couldn't be the killer at all. There were always exceptions to the rule, and maybe he was just stronger than he looked. Laura didn't have any connection between him and the victims yet, either, but then again, he hadn't given them any information at all. It might all still come together.

So why did she have the nagging feeling that it wasn't going to?

Toby Martins reached out for his cup of water again, whip-fast, and only succeeded in knocking it over. It spilled immediately, the rest of the water pooling on the table and dripping to the floor as the cup spun away. He went white in the face at the moment it happened, visibly swallowing, then again – his throat was clearly so dry he needed to do it twice.

63

Laura smiled to herself.

"Alright," she said. "You go and get another cup of water. Join me in a couple of seconds." She paused to pull a few tissues from a box that was sitting on the table beside the recording equipment and walked briskly into the interview room. She trusted that Agent Won would at least do as he was told without any problems, putting her game face back on as she returned to Toby Martins's direct line of view.

"Having a clumsy moment, Mr. Martins?" she said, as cheerfully as if she were a nurse doing the rounds with elderly patients. She stooped to pick up the cup, making sure to underline the fact that she was able to reach and move to get it while he was not, and then dumped the tissues on top of the water on the table. "Never mind. You can mop it up; there you go."

It was a power move in two directions: first, to make him clean up his own mess instead of doing it for him, and second, to remind him that he was being watched at all times. He didn't have any privacy here. That should help to keep him on edge, to increase his feelings of powerlessness and make him second guess everything.

All of which was going to help immensely with getting him to talk, even if he knew he shouldn't.

Laura sat in the chair opposite him and leaned back, crossing her arms over her chest – the way he clearly wanted to, but couldn't. She'd seen him try when they'd first left him in the room, finding the handcuffs too restrictive.

And then she simply looked at him while he reluctantly mopped up the spill, stopping it from spreading over the edge of the table and falling on his own legs, and heaped up the sopping wet tissues in a pile when he was done. Then he finally looked back at her, and glanced away, clearly uncomfortable.

Laura let the silence go on. The longer, the better, after all. She wasn't in any rush herself. Not while she still had the suspect right in front of her. If he was the one who had been doing this, then there was no way he could take another victim from here.

Of course, there was still that doubt in the back of her mind. But she shut it down. The point of the exercise was to make him lose control – not to freak herself out instead.

"How long are you going to keep me here?" he said, at last. That was a victory in itself. He'd been the first one to blink.

"It doesn't have to be much longer at all, Mr. Martins," Laura said. "All you have to do is answer our questions. Why did you run from us at the factory?"

Martins grunted. "Because I don't like pigs."

Laura allowed a small smile to quirk the corner of her mouth, to show him that she was more amused than insulted by his choice of epithet. "That might be a reason to avoid us. But you didn't just calmly avoid us, did you? You ran. You drove dangerously. It seemed like you were pretty desperate to get away from us."

"No comment," he said, apparently remembering that he was supposed to be sticking to the same technique.

Laura stretched out, catlike, getting comfortable in her chair. Where was Agent Won with that water? She hadn't imagined it would take him this long to bring it through. She'd wanted to use that, too, as an opportunity to break down Martins' barriers. Make him accept the grace of their drink, to soothe his aching throat. "Innocent people don't usually run from the law," she said, quoting an old line that was probably engraved into every cop's brain. Every cop who had ever dealt with a suspect who ran and then pretended it meant nothing, anyway.

Toby Martins said nothing, so neither did she. They simply sat there, opposite one another. He didn't like to look at her, she noticed. He couldn't meet her gaze. He shifted in his chair, uncomfortably. It was working. The silence. It was drawing him out. He was about to say...

The door opened, and Agent Won burst in. He wasn't holding a cup of water, like Laura had expected, but instead a brown file. Laura frowned at him. Not only had he interrupted the perfect moment – which, if she was being fair, he couldn't have known in advance – but he seemed to be going off-book yet again.

"I've just received a report from Detective Waters and the Captain," he said, putting the folder down on the table. He did it kind of recklessly, letting it slap down onto the surface somewhere between where Laura was sitting and where he would, before dropping into his chair. "They've just finished their search of Mr. Martins's property."

"Oh, really?" Laura asked, her interest piqued again. Maybe he had a good reason for defying her orders, after all. She picked up the folder, opening it at an angle so that only she could see the contents and Martins was none the wiser.

Which was a good job, really, because the pages inside the folder were blank.

"It's interesting reading," Agent Won said, pointing at the empty page as though there was something notable written there. "The sheer quantity of drug paraphernalia is quite impressive."

Laura raised an eyebrow as though she was reading the same interesting facts, deliberately letting her eyes scan from side to side to carry on the pretense. "I see that," she said. "What else did they find?"

Agent Won pointed a little further down the page, as if drawing her attention to a new paragraph. "A lot of equipment that came from the candle factory, by the looks of things. Chemicals, too. I think his employers are going to be very interested to hear about this."

"I don't doubt it," Laura said, nodding and smiling. She glanced up at Toby, who was watching them with a look of horror. "Feel inclined to answer any of our questions now? You might as well. It looks like we know enough to have you put away, anyway."

"I..." Martins swallowed, shaking his head. "I didn't think they'd miss any of it. And they didn't."

"So, you set up a small-scale drug manufacturing operation in your own home," Agent Won said. He was coming into his own a little, growing in confidence. Laura had to admit that she liked this side of him a little better than what she had seen so far. "Not the best of plans, was it? And how do the women fit into that? Did they find out?"

"The women? What women?" Martins said, shaking his head. There was a pause, and then his eyes widened. "The ones on the news that got killed? I don't know anything about that. It's nothing to do with me."

"You think we're going to accept that it's just a coincidence?" Agent Won scoffed. Laura didn't intervene. He was taking this in an interesting direction, to give him credit. She wasn't totally unreserved about the fact she might have to step in eventually, but for now... "Two women found dead with the candles from the place where you work? We already know you're stealing from the site. It seems ridiculous to assume you wouldn't take candles as well. And given your history of assault..."

"I didn't," Martins insisted, his eyes wide. "I wouldn't! I mean – hurt them! I wouldn't hurt them. They didn't do anything to me. I didn't take any candles either because I didn't need them. There wasn't any point in taking a risk by stealing something I didn't need and getting caught for all of it!"

66

"So, you admit you took the other items," Laura said, picking up on that point before the less experienced agent let it drop, only because it was such an important one.

"... Yes," Martins said, defeatedly, lowering his eyes. "Yes, I took them. But that was all. I never did anything else. I swear!"

"Where were you on Saturday night?" Laura asked. They needed to get right to the point.

"I was..." Martins stopped, looking down at the table. "I don't think I should say."

"You're already in enough trouble," Agent Won said, taking on a fatherly tone that was almost ridiculous given the difference in their ages. "The more open and honest you are with us now, the better it will go for you in front of the judge."

Martins hesitated still, then brought a hand up to his mouth, using his thumb to swipe across it as though he was trying to wipe his worries away. "I was in the parking lot next to the pebble beach," he muttered. "Selling."

Laura took a breath. If he was telling the truth, he had an alibi. It was an alibi that would be very difficult to prove, because few people would want to admit that they had seen him there. But then again, most people wouldn't admit to one major crime in order to give themselves an alibi for another.

"Can you prove it?" she asked.

Martins shook his head, but then glanced up. "I could give you the names of the people I was with."

Laura nodded. She closed the file with a snap, so that he would never know they'd been looking at nothing. "We'll leave you to talk to the police detectives about that," she said, getting up from her chair. She glanced at Agent Won to make sure he was following suit; he did. "Don't go clamming up again, Mr. Martins. You're putting yourself in a good position by admitting it all."

She left the room with that, allowing him time to digest those words. If they were the last thing ringing in his head when they sent the locals in to talk to him, hopefully it would help them to get a result.

Just not the result that they had hoped for in the first place.

"Do you believe him?" Agent Won asked, the moment the door was closed behind them.

Laura nodded, sighing. "Unfortunately, I do. He's an idiot and definitely a criminal, but he's not a killer."

"Are you sure?" Agent Won asked. He was practically pouting. "I was really certain…"

"I thought he was a pretty good candidate, too," Laura said, throwing him a bone. He hadn't done too badly in there, after all. "But that's how it is sometimes. The most likely suspect turns out to have an alibi. It just means there's another suspect out there we haven't caught yet."

Agent Won looked at his watch. "It's past ten," he said. "We were supposed to bring him in by now. The killer, I mean."

Laura nodded, accepting the uncomfortable truth. He was right. They'd had a deadline to work to, and they had most likely missed it.

"Let's just hope we're wrong about the pattern," she said. Even as she said it, though, she had a sinking feeling that they were about to get a call about a body left somewhere in town with a candle clutched tight to its chest.

CHAPTER TWELVE

Cici checked the time on her cell phone, almost groaning out loud at how slow the time was going. It was nearly the end of her shift, but it wasn't coming quickly enough. It never seemed to come quickly enough, and the more she checked the time, the more it seemed to slowly go.

"Can I get you anything?" she asked, brightening her face on purpose and trying to keep up that customer-friendly pep that the manager was always on her ass about. He was such a killjoy. And a Scrooge, too. She was pretty sure a pay raise was not in her foreseeable future.

The guy smiled back, pointing at the coffee machine behind her. "Can I get a coffee?" he asked. His usual request, whenever he came in. He had a bundle of items in his hands, too, and she'd seen him already pull up to the pumps outside. She rang up the coffee, the few things he'd picked out, and the pump total and then turned to make the coffee while he paid.

"Late one for you, tonight," she commented, since it was something to say. To fill the silence. He didn't reply – which she mostly expected anyway, since he was always so quiet. She glanced over her shoulder and saw him nod with a shy smile, acknowledging the truth of her words.

Well, okay then.

Cici placed the coffee down on the counter when the machine was done making it, trying to plaster on that smile again. It was difficult, sometimes. She tried to be nice, but when people were so introverted like this... if it wasn't for the fact that she had heard him say a few words here and there, she would have thought he didn't speak English or something.

"That's thirty dollars and seventeen cents total," she said, reading off the monitor of the till.

"Thank you," he said quietly, using his card to pay for it all and then starting to gather it up into his arms. He didn't bother asking for a bag. She was about to offer one, but it seemed almost strange to break the quiet of his presence again, and then he was turning and walking

69

away with everything held against his chest – except the coffee, in one outstretched hand.

There was no one else in the entirety of the gas station. Cici made a coffee for herself and sipped at it, blowing off the steam to try to cool it quicker, as she watched him walk back to his car and get inside. He settled all of his things down on the passenger seat under the illumination of the overheard light, put his coffee to one side in a holder, and then started his engine and drove away.

Well. Even a silent regular was better than no one at all. Cici sighed, taking another sip of the coffee. By the time she had finished this, her shift would be over, and she could make the walk home. She just had to hold off the crushing boredom until then.

She glanced around the inside of the store, seeing nothing that needed doing. The displays were all fine, and her incoming coworker, Chris, was a stickler for organization anyway. He loved doing that kind of thing. Given that he had the graveyard shift and would probably only serve a handful of people all night long, she wasn't going to take that away from him. She leaned over to swipe a magazine from the rack by the counter, reading a few pages without much interest. It was all celebrity gossip. Anything she was actually interested in, she had seen on social media already.

The opening of the gas station door made Cici jump, almost spilling the last mouthful of her coffee all over the magazine. She looked up and saw Chris and rolled her eyes at herself for being so jumpy.

"Hey!" he called out, heading over as she hastily stuffed the magazine back where it had come from. "Good shift."

"Mm," Cici said into the coffee cup as she finished it, throwing it right into the trash can after. "Just normal. Nothing out of the ordinary. Kinda slow towards the end."

"Yay," Chris said sarcastically, standing to the side to let her come out from behind the counter before he went in. "Sounds like good times for me. Well, have a good night."

"You, too," Cici said, smiling briefly. She paused in front of the counter to take off her nametag and slide on a jacket against the cold, holding her purse between her knees, before grabbing it again and slinging it over her shoulder. "See you for changeover tomorrow."

"See you then," Chris nodded, with that kind of grimly humorous look that only two employees in a dead-end job can share.

Cici walked out into the night, shuddering as the first breath of cold air ghosted across her skin. It was definitely bracing. But at this time of night there were no buses, and even if there had been one, it was free to walk home. Cici wasn't trying to spend all of her aggressively low paycheck on unnecessary things like the bus, even if it was cold. The walk would get the blood flowing and warm her up.

She wrapped her arms around herself, holding the jacket closer as she stepped out of the range of the gas station's lights and into the darkness. She knew the way back by heart at this point, including the shortcut across the field by the station and the exact angle to take in order to avoid tripping over some of the artfully placed rocks from the shore. She took a deep breath, smelling the ocean on the breeze. It was nice sometimes to remember that she had it good, living somewhere like this. Not everyone got to work a dead-end job in a beautiful place like Pacific Cove.

It was a still, calm night. She could hear the crunching of her own footsteps as she walked across the grass and stones, see her breath pooling white in front of her. While her face was cold, at least the rest of her was wrapped up, and her hands were tucked in under her upper arms. It wasn't unpleasant at all. In fact, without the headlights of cars on the road, it was pretty peaceful. The kind of night where you can look up and admire the stars, which she did.

There was a crunch behind her, and Cici whipped her head around, staring back into the gloom.

She could see the lights of the gas station in the distance, already far enough away that they were getting smaller. Between her and there, there was no sign of a silhouette, nothing blocking out the lights. She paused anyway, looking carefully, her heart racing. Hadn't she heard a footstep?

She turned back and carried on walking, telling herself she was being stupid. It was probably a rabbit, or something. Some little nocturnal animal making its way out for the night or coming home after a long day of whatever it was little animals did. She walked a bit quicker, all the same. It was a good reminder that she was totally in the dark out here, unaware of her surroundings. She started kicking her legs forward a bit as she walked, too – she knew from hard-earned experience that it was far less painful to hit the end of her boot on an unexpected rock than to trip over it.

She really needed to calm down. It was probably that coffee she'd had so close to the end of her shift, but Cici couldn't shake this awful feeling that she was being watched. Followed. She became so aware of her own movements, of what they would look like to someone who was observing her. She didn't want to look like she was scared.

But she kind of was.

Cici's senses were all on alert suddenly, making every moment heightened. She could swear that she could hear the distant humming of the gas station lights, even though she was so far away now she hadn't even noticed it before. Somewhere out on the coastal road, around the bend and out of sight, the swish of a car's tires on the road. The small noises of a few birds out in the distance, maybe over the water. And the water itself, distant but there, always there no matter where you went in town.

And above it all, the sound of her own urgent breathing and her rapid heartbeat pounding in her ears.

Cici walked faster, thinking it would be better anyway if she got home fast. It was getting colder than she had expected, after all. She half-turned her head to the right again, looking over her shoulder, straining for something…

And to her left, there was a rustle.

Like someone had suddenly darted to the side and into a bush to avoid being seen as she turned.

Cici was done waiting to find out if she was right about someone being there. She rushed forward, breaking into a jog across the grass, very aware even as she did so that there was every chance she would stumble and fall if she didn't take enough caution. She fumbled for her cell phone in her pocket: the light would show anyone who was around exactly where she was, yes, but if they already knew then she had nothing to lose from seeing the way ahead of herself. She needed to see. She needed to get out of here and back onto the road, and in sight of other people driving by if there were any. And if not, then home, home as fast as she could run.

She was just managing to get it out of her pocket when something caught her – something right around her waist, like she'd run into something – heavy and hard – no, flexible – an arm –

Someone had grabbed her around the waist, arresting her motion and plucking her right out of the air, pulling her back towards them.

There was something over her mouth, too, something she realized when she tried to take a breath and couldn't. Cici's lungs fought the unnatural feeling, immediately going to take a second deep breath through her nose and mouth, and all she got was a sweet smell that

72

reminded her somehow of the hospital. It filled her senses entirely, a poor substitute for air, and...

And...

Cici fought to hold on, to grasp the train of thought. She could smell the sweetness, and her head felt dizzy, and her legs – her legs were gone, and...

Cici spiraled down into darkness, losing track of everything, consciousness pulling away from her like a silk scarf caught by the wind.

***

He carried her gently, taking the care and time that she deserved. She was a precious burden, and he did not resent the weight. She was limp in his arms, lifeless now. It was funny: they always seemed to be so much heavier than he expected

It was just difficult to carry her head and support it properly, not letting it loll back and open up her wound even further.

Pacific Cove was so dead at night. No pun intended by that, of course, but he had always noticed it. He was the kind of man who liked to walk in the solitude, to enjoy the quiet. He always had been. It was nicer, sometimes, to walk around here without anyone else to spoil it. To judge you, or make you feel judged. To try to talk to you, when you didn't have the words to make the small talk they expected.

On balance, he would rather be around people, but the quiet of the night had plenty of advantages too. And this was one of them: taking his time, giving Cici the respect and care that she deserved. Making sure that she found her final placement without being interrupted.

He had chosen the spot carefully. He didn't like to move too far from the first place he had found them; it seemed more respectful to keep them close, to let them take their rest as soon as possible. And this spot was a good one, even if not quite as good as the last. There had to be a certain amount of compromise. He wouldn't have risked walking all the way back to the marketplace tonight, so this spot had to be the one.

He laid her down gently, supporting her head to the last and then smoothing out her hair, letting it fan around her head like she was a princess in a book. Which she was, of course. She was a princess to him. Now, no one would ever be able to treat her otherwise.

He laid a hand on her forehead carefully for a moment, as if to make sure that she was resting as peacefully as she could. Then he arranged her arms, crossing them over on her chest so that they formed a kind of cup, a space where the candle could sit without falling. Rigor mortis was only just beginning to set in, but once it was complete, she would hold the candle still and safe. It would be quick enough now that he knew he could set her up and leave her, letting her take the same rest as the others.

He placed the candle where it needed to be and tightened her arms just a little, checking his work. She looked peaceful. Content, even. Perfect. She was never again going to be at risk of losing this. As she was now, so she would be forever in the memories of those who knew her. Young, beautiful, and perfect. That was a part of it all, a gift that he hoped would satisfy them as they looked down on him and what he had done from above.

It was time to light the candle. He stood reverentially above her to take out the box of matches from his pocket, selecting one in the dim light that seemed to be a good fit. He struck it against the side of the box until it flared into life, a burst of orange which pushed the darkness backwards.

He stooped to light the candle and touched the match to the wick, waiting for it to catch. When it did, he drew away slowly, making sure that it had stuck and wasn't going to blow out immediately.

He cursed, shaking his hand in the air as he dropped the match, feeling the burn on his fingers. It had only been for a moment, and he suspected there was no real damage, but the match was gone into the darkness, skittering across the ground and going out before he had a chance to see where it had landed. It was somewhere outside the small circle of light cast by the candle; he could lift the candle now to check for it, but that would mean taking it out of Cici's hands, and it was burning already, and he might not be able to get it back in if he did that.

He crouched low, brushing his fingers over the ground, feeling the rough surface and trying to identify one thing that should not be there. But before he found it, he heard voices nearby – voices coming back, no doubt, to one of the cars parked around him.

The match was gone, and he wasn't going to find it before they reached him.

He had to decide whether to let it go – and fast.

With one last internal curse, he cast a last glance at the floor and, seeing nothing, started to run on swift and quiet feet as far as he could get from the glow of Cici's candle.

CHAPTER THIRTEEN

Laura slouched in the chair she had been given, trying to rest her lower back. There was nothing like a long flight and a long day on a case to give you an ache that wouldn't stop.

"Where else do we look?" Agent Won asked. He was back to being grumbly, acting like he couldn't sit still. The boy obviously wanted to shoot off and take action on some other front. Not for the first time and almost certainly not for the last, Laura missed Nate with a deep-seated ache in her chest. If he was here, he would be thinking of ways to attack the problem alongside her, not waiting for her lead.

"Check over the employee records," Laura suggested. She had little hope it would yield anything else, if the locals had already looked, but it was something for Agent Won to do. "Maybe look for something that isn't obvious. Someone missing work when they were supposed to be in over the last few days, for example, or being late for their shift. Or leaving early. Even someone who booked an off holiday. Those kinds of things."

"Okay," Agent Won sighed, with a tone in his voice that suggested he wasn't as fooled by her attempt to keep him busy as she'd hoped he would be.

She could worry about whether she was hurting his feelings later. Right now, she needed to put her own thinking cap on and figure this out. The candle factory was a bust, it seemed – Toby Martins had been processed and was under arrest for a number of drug and theft charges, but that had nothing to do with their case. It might have been exciting for the locals, who didn't see much of those types of cases, but their excitement was short-lived too. There was a kind of pall hanging over the small office – too small to even call it a bullpen – where Laura and Agent Won had been allowed to set up shop.

Laura tried to think, knitting her brows together. The candle. What did the candle mean? She knew it had to have something to do with her vision. What did the placement in public spaces mean? There had to be a meaning behind it, something that Laura hadn't grasped yet. Exhibition? Or care?

The blood, too – the blood had to go somewhere, because the throats were clearly cut at a different location. And what about the fact he had knocked them out first? That had to be a link they could follow, tracking down who had purchased large quantities of the drug required. Then again, Toby Martins had just effectively demonstrated that the drug trade in Pacific Cove wasn't exactly under control. Maybe that, too, would be hard to trace.

She had to start somewhere. Laura took a breath, ultimately deciding on –

A sharp crackle cut through the air, a dispatch radio on a desk lighting up and blaring out a message.

"All units, all units, we have a ten-one-hundred. Parking lot by the gas station on Ocean View Boulevard. Please respond."

Ten-one-hundred. Laura knew that code.

A dead body had been found.

It was like the feeling of a train slamming into her at full speed. Another body. Another failure. They'd let someone down in the worst possible way tonight. Laura closed her eyes only for a moment, because a moment was all she had before they had to get moving.

"Won," she hissed, leaping out of her chair and grabbing his arm to make him follow. He dropped his paperwork in a rush as Laura nodded at Detective Waters and his partner, indicating for them to come along with. They would need a guide. Someone to take them to the scene as quickly as possible. Following a police car with its lights and siren blaring would help immensely with that.

But no matter how quickly they got there, Laura knew: they'd run out of time. They'd failed. The killer had struck again, and they hadn't been able to stop him.

***

It was dark still as they descended on the scene, casting the parking lot in the unnatural red and blue glow of the police lights. There were a couple of civilians huddled at one side, near a parked car; in front of them, unmistakable even in the gloom, was the body.

With the candle still lit.

Laura jumped out of the car practically in the same motion as switching the engine off, and Agent Won was already ahead of her. They raced over, beating Detective Waters and his partner – who seemed reluctant to even approach now. She couldn't say she blamed them. She was sure it would hit different when you were walking up to see the body of someone you knew. Being an FBI agent had that anonymity to its advantage.

Laura took in the scene as much as she could in the moment, wanting to preserve it in her head. There was one light at the far end of the parking lot, high up and powerful enough to cast just enough glow to be able to see by, though it was a pale kind of seeing. The kind that the moon could provide on clear nights: everything bathed in a strange monochrome. The body lay on the ground, placed just so, the hair fanned out around the head and the limbs positioned straight. She was holding a candle, like the others. It had been long enough for some drops of wax to run down the side of the candle and onto her hands. Her eyes were closed, as though she was only sleeping.

Laura had to admit there was a strange kind of beauty to the scene. A peace. The body looked as though it was meant to be here, even if it was totally incongruous in the middle of a parking lot. Laura got down onto her knees beside the body, ducking her head to examine it as much as she could. Was there any sign here? Anything that she should be seeing? Anything that, so far, she had missed?

"Detective Waters?" she called out. He moved to her side with a slow kind of reverence. He did not seem unhurried, but only solemn in the presence of the body.

He seemed to know what she was asking before she had to voice it more clearly. "I recognize her. It's Cecilia Powers. She works at the gas station."

Laura looked up in the direction he was pointing, to see a gas station in the distance. Close enough that she could make out the lights, far enough that she had no hope of reading the signage. It looked like an island in the darkness. Between here and there it was all black, nothing illuminating it at all.

"I want you to do these three things, in order," she said, keeping her voice calm so he would listen and obey. "First, call the station and get everyone else down here after us. Second, talk to our two witnesses over there and get them to tell you everything they saw. If they saw a person around here at all, you need to come get me so I can hear it for myself. And third, when everyone else arrives, we need a scene of crime established from here all the way back to the gas station. Everything needs locking down and cordoning off – no one crosses this area until we've done a thorough search. Got it?"

"Got it," Detective Waters said. He sounded unbearably sad. He lingered a moment longer. "She was just a normal girl. Lived here for years with her family. I've been served by her more times than I can count."

"I'm sorry, Detective," Laura said softly. She looked up at him in the gloom. His eyes hadn't left Cecilia's face. "Now, please. Do what I've asked, and let's get her some justice – and stop this from happening again."

That did the trick. Waters moved off, leaving only Won on the other side of the body. He had crouched too, trying to see what he could see.

"Should I blow out the candle?" he asked.

"Yes," Laura said. "Carefully, though. We don't want to contaminate any evidence."

She got back to her feet as he did so. She could already see that this body was just like the other two. They would wait for the report from the coroner to confirm it, of course, but it looked like she had been through the same process: knocked out, throat cut and drained, moved here to be put on display with the candle.

It was ghoulish. But there was something more to it. Something about the way she had been placed. And there was some kind of connection between the three victims so far, too: they had all worked in jobs that allowed them to interact with members of the public, in customer-facing roles. Serving. Was that something? Laura couldn't tell yet, but it stood out to her. There had to be something here.

"It's late," she said. "He's already struck again, so we can't save anyone else tonight, and we're going to have to wait for the coroner's report to learn anything new from her body. I don't think we should talk to the family right away, not when they're going to have to digest this news. And to be honest, I don't even know how much use they'll be. It's becoming clearer that this, whatever it is, isn't just some personal vendetta against the victims themselves. If it was, we'd have dug something up by now. A rumor, at least."

"What if people don't know about the link?" Agent Won asked, standing back up to her level.

"In a small town like this?" Laura scanned the horizon, the darkness, the faint glow in the distance where one or two properties – likely on main street – still had their lights on. "People talk. And we haven't heard anything. Anyway, my point is, as much as I hate to say it, we need to get some sleep."

79

Wasn't this a turn up for the books? It was normally Nate having to tell Laura not to push herself too far, reminding her that humans need sleep to function and to think properly. Now she was the one doing it. Things were upside down, and she hated it.

"Alright," Agent Won shrugged, apparently not in any big rush to get back to the case like she would have been in most situations. "I'll go look up the motel's address so we can find it on the GPS."

Laura nodded distantly, letting him go. She took one more look down at Cecilia Powers, who was still lying in that same peaceful position. It was far from peaceful, really, she knew. But there was something about it. Something she couldn't yet put her finger on.

Laura turned to go, but as she did, something caught her eye. The beams of the car headlights, left on when they'd both parked, were striking the ground nearby; and there was something there. Something small, like a twig of some kind, only about a quarter inch long. Laura stooped to pick it up, bringing it closer to her face in the gloom to examine it – or try to. It was blackened, twisted. She couldn't see much from it in the darkness, but –

"Agent Frost?" Agent Won called out. "I've got the car set up. We can go."

Laura nodded, turning around to show him that she'd heard, and then took an evidence bag out of her inside jacket pocket. She always had one or two in there, just in case. She tucked the twig away, not knowing exactly why, but feeling like she should.

She walked over to the car to get inside, her mind already on the morning and what it would bring. More clues, she hoped, though she wasn't exactly optimistic. And while her visions seemed to have no trouble coming through right now, they weren't at all useful; seeing flames being snuffed out really gave her nothing, which probably meant they had so far come nowhere close at all to catching their killer.

If he stayed on target with his timeline, they had another forty-eight hours before they would be standing at another crime scene just like this one, blowing out a candle placed on top of another dead local girl. And if he didn't stick to the same rules, perhaps because he was escalating or because he knew the FBI were on the case and wanted to get his timeline moving along quicker, then it could be a lot less. That meant that every second counted.

Wasting so many of them asleep weighed on Laura's conscience, as it always did – but there was little for them to do.

With a good night's sleep, space to think, and distance, Laura was confident her investigative brain was going to kick in where her psychic brain had failed her.

And if it didn't?

It was going to be a long two days before she got any rest again.

CHAPTER FOURTEEN

Laura stretched her stiff muscles over her head, trying to work out the kinks with the sea breeze in her nose. It was a different kind of way to wake up, a little nicer than the class of motel they were used to. It seemed there was no such thing as an absolute dive in Pacific Cove – even the cheapest option the FBI was willing to shell out for had comfortable beds and an ocean view.

None of which mattered at all, because you had to actually sleep in those comfortable beds to get the benefit of them, and Laura had hardly been able to. She'd tossed and turned all night, waking fitfully from dreams of unseen killers putting candles on girls and lighting them on fire. Like her subconscious was trying to tell her something – just not something that actually gave her any insight.

She was still struggling to see the connection between the victims, and it irked her that she hadn't found it yet. Three was a charm, though. And maybe, she thought, Cecilia Powers's family would be able to help her figure it out. She wasn't ruling out the potential of their testimony just yet.

She moved to the room next door and knocked on it, waiting for Agent Won to answer. It was early still, but the sun was rising, and that meant it was time to go. Part of the reason for her sleepless night had been the fact that she knew the killer was still out there. Maybe looking for his victim even now. She knew from the initial reports that the first victims were killed only within an hour of being found, but that didn't mean he couldn't change things up. That was the worst, scariest part about working cases like these: never knowing when the rug would be pulled out from under your feet, when it would be too late again.

There was no answer from Agent Won. Laura moved to the side, to the small window with its quaint lacy curtains and white-painted frame. Cupping her hands around her head, she could just about see the floor of the room through the lace, though nothing more than that.

What she did see was a pair of black suit pants left lying on the floor, and a couple of discarded men's shoes beside them. Agent Won was definitely not dressed. She paused a moment, listening, putting her ear closer to the door.

82

She heard a faint snoring, and almost rolled her eyes right back into her head with the force of how it hit her. He was still asleep.

Damn rookies.

Laura sighed, shaking her head to herself. Her options were few. She could either wake him and wait for him to get ready before she started her day, which could take a while – or she could just get on with it and leave him to catch up later.

It would be a good lesson, she thought. That if you slept in you got left behind. Next time, he could set an alarm, make sure he was awake at an appropriate time. She nodded to herself at this decision, turning to get into their rental car alone.

She looked at her cell phone as she started the engine, waiting for the car to warm up just a touch. It was chilly outside, and while she did enjoy the bracing nature of it, it wasn't comfortable for long. She scrolled through her conversation with Nate – if you could call it a conversation; lately it was just her asking him to call her, over and over again, begging him to talk about his transfer. There still had been no reply. No sign that he had even thought about trying to contact her.

And then there was one message on her phone, one that made her bite her lip. It was from Chris, telling her he was looking forward to seeing her tonight if she was back in the state. The question mark at the end of the text message let her know that he was expecting an answer, but she couldn't give him one. Not just yet.

If she said something now, it would be no. She'd have to cancel. And she didn't want to do that. She wanted to get this case solved before lunchtime, jump on a plane, and get back to Washington, D.C., in time to have dinner with him. It was selfish, she knew. But she'd been looking forward to their date.

And if she got back in time for that date, then no one else would die, which was just about the bonus to end all bonuses.

Laura pulled out of the parking lot and drove the admittedly short distance to the precinct – Agent Won would be able to simply walk over when he finally woke up. And when he did, he would find Laura gone, because her plan was to just pick up the information from the local department and then drive right on over to find the Powers family, whoever they might have been.

She went through the motions, putting the car where it needed to be and then getting out and walking through the precinct with her head firmly on the case. She was having trouble with the job connection between the three girls. There was a kind of disconnect that she was struggling to understand. First of all, it seemed like the fact that they all worked public-facing jobs meant that anyone could have been the killer. It could be someone that they encountered on their daily rounds, someone they just met one time. Someone that was a customer for years. There was no real way to know.

It might have been that they had a stalker, just like Colt Peake. Someone who went around following them, but maybe not so obvious as Peake had been. Or maybe it was just someone who lived in the town and had snapped, and went after those who were very visible to him. The fact that they were interacting with the public on such a regular basis, every day of their working lives, meant that it even could be a tourist or someone who was simply passing through. No personal connection, just a crime of opportunity.

But then again... The candles, the way he laid them out in these public places. It was at once a performance meant to be seen, and an intimate display of affection. Maybe. Laura felt like she was going around and around in her head, unable to really settle on a clear definition of the killer's behavior. Just from the MO of the way the bodies were left, she would normally have assumed that the killings were very personal. Deeply so.

But then, the rest of it just didn't add up. And there didn't seem to be any clear personal connection between all three of the women. Sure, they lived in the same town, but so far it seemed as though they didn't even run in the same circles. But there again, she doubted herself, wondering if she had missed something. It was a small town, after all. Everyone knew everyone. So, someone must have been the missing link between the three.

As she approached the desk she had been sitting at yesterday, Laura spotted a file that had been popped on top of it by one of the local detectives. It was a dossier with all of the information about Cecilia Powers and her family, and she snatched it up gratefully. She took the time only to wave it in the air, making sure that at least one person still sitting in the office had seen her taking it to indicate that she was going, and then she left. She didn't want to hang around even further.

She got back into the car and started the engine again, setting up the GPS as her mind replayed mentally those visions she had seen. First flames, then flames being snuffed out. Was it a literal vision? Was it a vision of the past, like she'd had recently for the very first time? How was she supposed to know anymore? Was it even some kind of

84

metaphor? Not the vision itself, but whatever the killer was doing - did he think that it symbolized something different?

She needed the answers – but it was starting to feel like all she had were questions.

***

Laura looked up at a warning from the GPS, and realized that she'd managed to drive all the way to the house of Cecilia Powers's mother on autopilot, just obeying the instructions from the machine and barely even thinking about it. She was distracted, but at least she was distracted by the case. She was going to get to the bottom of this, she told herself. She had to.

She knocked on the door with that trepidation that always came from approaching the family of the deceased. Knowing they were going through the worst thing that had ever happened to them, and now she had to march right in there and basically interrogate them. But it couldn't be avoided. As far as she knew, no one had officially interviewed Mrs. Powers yet – there was nothing about it in the file she'd been left. She guessed the locals had been waiting for her to make that decision, and she couldn't really blame them.

It was the kind of job you didn't take on unless you had to.

Mrs. Powers answered the door with a tissue clutched in her hands, fresh tear tracks on her cheeks. Instead of getting dressed, it looked as though she'd got out of bed last night and thrown on a robe, and that was how she still was.

"Are you with the police?" she asked immediately, and Laura braced herself, wondering whether she was going to get *thank God you're here* or *why the hell aren't you doing anything?*

"I'm with the FBI, ma'am," Laura said. "My name is Special Agent Laura Frost. I want to ask you some questions about your daughter, if now is a good time for you."

It was really just a nicety – she had to ask the questions. If the woman said no, it would make everything a whole lot more complicated. But Laura did like to ask, because it put things on a more equal footing. She was seeking permission, not just telling the woman it had to happen. That made the grieving families more at ease in most cases, even if it didn't manifest in their behavior right away.

"Come in," Mrs. Powers said, turning and leading her down a hallway. It was stuffed with photographs: pictures of Cecilia in life, as

85

a child and then a teen and then a young woman, family portraits with a man who must be her father, Mrs. Powers herself at various stages of her life. They must have been a close, loving family.

Only Mrs. Powers was listed in the dossier Laura had been given. One left out of three. She wondered where the father was, and whether he would be significant in any way.

"Thank you," Laura said, as she settled into a chair to Mrs. Powers's left, as the woman herself sat down on a sofa. The living room held more photographs, beside the furniture and a large-screen television. It all looked nice enough, if a few years old. "I'm sorry for your loss, and that we have to do this now. But we'd really like to catch this person before anyone else gets hurt."

Mrs. Powers nodded. She lifted her chin up, like she was trying to be brave. "Please. Ask whatever you need to."

Laura nodded. "This first question may be hard to contemplate. But I want you to think really hard. Is there anyone you can think of who might have wanted to harm your daughter, in any way? Even if you think that something like this would be a total overreaction?"

Mrs. Powers sat, looking up at the ceiling with red-rimmed eyes, like she was trying to think. Laura saw the lines of her daughter's face in the mother's. A resemblance that would no doubt haunt her, now, when she looked in the mirror. "No," she said at length. Laura had the impression she really had taken the time to think about it deeply, which was something. But it was still nothing, after all. "No, there's no one I can think of."

"Your daughter still lived here, isn't that right?" Laura asked, going off the information she'd read.

"Yes, she's only twenty-one," Mrs. Powers said. Her face crumpled a little as she seemed to realize what she'd said: *is*, not *was*.

Laura made a mental note of that. She hadn't processed the thought until now, but Cecilia was the youngest victim so far. In fact, each of the victims had descended in age exactly: twenty-three, twenty-two, twenty-one. Was that something? Could she follow that link, start isolating any twenty-year-old women who lived in town? Maybe it was worth a shot. Or maybe she was just grasping at straws.

"What about her father?" Laura asked delicately, phrasing the question as openly as possible. Mrs. Powers could interpret it as she would and offer the most logical answer that came to her. That was probably better than going direct and getting it wrong.

"He passed about five years ago," Mrs. Powers said. She looked at Laura with a kind of misty sadness in her eyes, a pain that was long held but still burned. "Cancer."

For a moment, Laura couldn't even find the words. To be widowed, and then to lose a child. It was awful. "I'm sorry," she said, at last. At least there was nothing to follow up there. No jealous jilted parent, no suspicious circumstances surrounding two generations of deaths. She paused respectfully before continuing. "Do you know if Cecilia spent any time with either Evelina Collins or Ashley Christianson?"

"She knew Ashley," Mrs. Powers nodded. "She never mentioned Evelina, though they went to the same school. She was a couple of years younger. Maybe just a bit too much of an age gap for them to have connected. She hadn't gone to college, my Cici. A lot of her old friends around here drifted away from her, anyway, because they went out of town. Even if they came back, it wasn't quite the same anymore."

Laura nodded sympathetically. "Do you know if she had a boyfriend, or any exes?"

"A couple," Mrs. Powers said vaguely. "But they were nice boys. I don't always remember their names... it wasn't ever serious, I don't think."

Laura wished she could get a more definitive answer, but she could see the woman was doing her best. She was starting to drift away into the grief again, to be consumed by it. Laura needed to wrap things up, to ask her final questions fast before it was too late.

"Do candles mean anything to you?" she asked, since it was worth a try.

"Candles?" Mrs. Powers said, with a sweet but sad smile. "She loved candles."

Laura sat up straighter. "Cici did?"

"I can show you," Mrs. Powers said, getting up. It seemed to take her an age to do so, struggling against the softness of the sofa, pushing herself to her feet. Laura was on the verge of reaching out a helping hand when Mrs. Powers managed it and began to amble away, down the hall again.

Laura followed her to a door which was decorated with cutout butterflies, layered on top of one another for a 3D effect. The door of a teenager's bedroom, still kept the same way since she'd never left home. Mrs. Powers pushed it open and led Laura inside, into a room that was neatly kept and somewhere awkward between child and adult, a space that must have contained so many memories within its walls.

The sheets on the bed were neutral toned, silk, very mature and grown-up. The books on the shelves, though, were those of a teenager's library – young adult titles about vampires and werewolves and gossipy intrigue. The wardrobe, hanging open, contained workwear and formalwear next to miniskirts and cropped tees. Even the walls were a mishmash of inspirational quotes in solemn frames and glossy photographs of young friends, some of them crinkled or faded with time.

But over and above it all, dominating almost every surface, were the candles.

They were all shapes and sizes, most of them in decorated containers that held labels denoting their scent. Half-baked cookie, vanilla cheesecake, fresh brownie – they sounded more like a café menu than candles. Laura stepped closer and picked one up, looking at it and bringing it to her nose. The scent of birthday cake brought a headache with it, making her stop and examine the label more closely –

Flames. Flames all around her, filling her sight until it was the only thing she could comprehend. And then a flash, a split second, and the flames were gone – blown or snuffed out.

Laura blinked. The same vision. First the fire, and then it was gone. What did it mean? Why was she seeing things twice now?

"She loved buying them," Mrs. Powers said. "Burning them, too. I always had to watch her closely to make sure she didn't leave one on when she went to sleep or left the house. It was a fire hazard, I used to say, but she never paid me any attention. She just loved the smell of them."

Laura turned the candle over, looking at the bottom. There was a brief description written there: *made in China* stood out to her. It wasn't one of the candles made at the local factory. She scanned across the room, looking for anything with a different label. "Did she always buy this brand?" Laura asked.

Mrs. Powers nodded. "My Tony, he used to buy them for her as birthday gifts. She loves them. She always keeps the same brand because she remembers him by them."

Laura chewed her lip for a moment, thinking. She put the candle back, letting her fingers stray across the one next to it just in case something else would be triggered. There was nothing. For all she knew, she was just getting a vision of what was destined to happen to the candle itself, at this point. It wouldn't be the first time a vision had turned out to be totally unconnected to a case in any way.

The candles weren't the same type as the ones the killer used – the long-burning, thick kind, plain and white with no scent. They were seemingly unconnected. Just another clue that didn't quite add up. Laura felt like screaming.

"Thank you, Mrs. Powers," she said. "You've been very helpful. If something else comes to mind, I want you to call me, okay? No matter what it might be."

Laura checked her watch as she left the property, heading back to the car. It was still early in the morning, but she could already feel time slipping away from her. She needed to get back to the precinct and figure out her next steps – and try not to panic about the fact that she really had no idea what to do next.

CHAPTER FIFTEEN

Laura walked in through the doors of the precinct and clocked Agent Won immediately. He was sitting at the desk they had been assigned – well, not at it, but *on* it, apparently holding court with three of the local detectives. He was talking something over with them, expressing himself with his hands – which made her feel very nervous indeed.

She wished she didn't have to feel quite so much like a babysitter, but there it was.

"Agent Won," she called out, as she headed into the room. She could have added some kind of catty remark, like *nice of you to join us*, but she held her tongue. She could make him feel guilty for sleeping in on their own time. Putting him down in front of other officers wasn't right.

"Oh, Agent Frost," he said, turning and quickly leaping down from the desk. "I was just discussing with Frank, Steve, and Mandy here about the possibility of a new angle."

Laura tilted her head, coming to a stop in front of him. "Well," she said. "Let's hear it." She had nothing to lose, after all. Talking to Mrs. Powers had been something of a bust – more confusing than anything else.

"Fire," he said, triumphantly, as if it explained everything.

Laura raised an eyebrow at him.

"Well," Agent Won said, hastily, clearly excited about his idea. "The killer likes candles, right? He likes lighting the flame. It's always burning when we get there, and I think that's significant."

"I'm sure it is," Laura agreed, though what she wasn't sure about was that they were on the same page.

"I think he likes fire in particular," Agent Won said. "Most killers usually graduate from smaller, more petty crimes into murder, right? And pyromania is quite common among serial killers. I think that's what we're dealing with, here. He's a pyromaniac, and he lights the candle because he can't resist adding a touch of flame to his murders as well."

90

Laura turned it over in her head, glancing at the cops behind Agent Won. They all looked fairly eager, like they were buying into it and wanted to get started on the investigation in this direction. It was easy to get swept up in the excitement of a new theory, especially when you didn't have one to begin with. They were probably also pretty excited about getting something to work on from an FBI agent, given that they didn't see many big cases down here.

But all that didn't mean that Laura couldn't also see where he was coming from. She thought about her vision of the flames – something she couldn't share, but it did back up Agent Won's theory. It could even be possible that was what the visions were trying to tell her – to look for someone who was obsessed with the flames.

But, still…

"It's a good theory," she conceded. "But why doesn't he bring fire into it more? Why not light the bodies on fire to hide the evidence of his crimes, or burn down the places where he took them?"

Agent Won's confident expression faltered a little, dropping from his face as he tried to answer the question. "Maybe because the killing is separate from the arson. You know? Like, two different crimes. It's just a little touch he likes to add."

Laura couldn't say his answer was too convincing. "And yet you think the candle is enough evidence to be sure that he's a pyromaniac?"

"Well," Agent Won hesitated, looking more uncertain than ever now. "Well, not, like, *sure*. But, I mean, it's something, right?"

Laura considered it for another long moment, leaving him hanging. "The way I see it, the commission of the murders themselves has very little to do with fire," she said. "There's no sign of burning of the bodies, no burning at the sight – the only thing we have is the candle. And for all we know right now, maybe the use of the candle is about wax, or about time, or something completely distinct from the flame. But… in the absence of anything else, yes, it's something."

A beam broke out on Agent Won's face. He looked so much like a little boy being given praise by a father figure that Laura almost faltered in her resolve to resent having to work with him. It was almost adorable. It was a shame that being adorable wasn't exactly a required trait for an FBI agent, however.

"We should start looking into it right away, like I was saying," Agent Won said, spinning around to face the other detectives again.

"Have there been any local arson reports recently?" Laura asked. "We wouldn't have to be talking whole properties on fire – even just unattended flames, garbage cans set on fire, little brushfires, anything."

The officers shook their heads, looking to each other for confirmation. "We didn't have any suspicions of someone like that in the area before now," one of them – the woman, and therefore most likely Mandy – said. "But we didn't think we had a murderer either and here we are."

Laura nodded. That was a sensible approach to take: assume that all of your assumptions until now were faulty. "Well, you'll need to look into the records of anyone who now lives in the area," she said. "Starting from maybe five or even ten years ago, you need to compile lists of anyone who was ever accused of starting a fire – and especially those who had it confirmed. These won't all necessarily be arrests – you might have fines on record, for example. If you can't find anyone in your own arrest and fine logs, then start looking at people who've moved from out of town recently."

There was a general murmur of agreement and a lot of nodding heads as the detectives began to disperse back to their own desks. Agent Won looked unaccountably pleased with himself, following them to stand over one of their monitors and observe as they presumably brought up their internal system.

Four cooks toiling over one dish was already enough, and Laura knew her talents would not be best used in simply doing the same thing as them. She chewed her lip for a moment in thought, and then turned on the computer they'd been assigned, making up her mind. While they looked at arrest records and individuals, she could look into this pyromancy thing from another angle. Incidents and fires. Arson wasn't always solved or even detected, and that meant there might be more out there the records couldn't tell them about.

Laura searched for and navigated to the page of a local newspaper. With the simple keyword 'fire,' she began to trawl back through their records, looking for anything that would stand out.

Of course, there were plenty of things that didn't have any relevancy at all. A Firefly Dance barn raiser. News about the local fire department, that was more to do with the arrival of a new captain or fundraising events than actual fires. But there were fires, here and there, and Laura read into each of them, jotting down the details.

The articles seemed to be filtered by relevancy rather than by date, which was irritating, but Laura fought through it. On the third page of the results, she spotted something: a fire that was dated very recently. She clicked open the article and read through it, her interest growing with every second.

LOCAL STORE LOST TO FLAMES

Lighting The Way, a store which opened five years ago on West Ocean Drive, has been burned to the ground in a terrible accident which has devastated the owner.

Michael Noran, 53, spoke to our reporter on what was once the grounds of his well-stocked and recently refurbished store. He said: "I just can't believe this has happened. Obviously, on some level you always know that you're dealing with a very flammable product, but I never expected something like this to happen. It's my whole life's work really, just gone, just like that. It's the end of a dream."

The fire was reported at 4 A.M. on Saturday morning, just a few hours before Lighting The Way was set to open for the weekend's trading. The store, which was in a central location on West Ocean Drive and popular with tourists, was fully stocked with scented candles and other themed items, such as essential oils, burners, and incense sticks. Firefighters say that the stock would have caught fire quickly, turning a small accidental flame into an inferno which ravaged the building and ultimately brought it down before anything could be done to save it.

When asked if he would rebuild and reopen the store, Noran was only able to look down at the blackened ash and remains of his store and shake his head sadly.

The Pacific Cove fire chief and police chief came together to issue this joint statement to all homeowners in the town: "This is a timely reminder that fire is dangerous and is not something to be played with. If you are burning candles in the home, please make sure that all flames are snuffed out before leaving the room or falling asleep. This is also a good time to check that your fire alarm is functional – it could save your life."

Laura felt a smile coming over her face, in spite of herself. A fire at a candle store. Not only was it the kind of delicious irony that would probably make it onto some kind of wacky world news round-up site, but it was also extremely relevant.

"Agent Won," she called out. "Get your jacket. I have a lead. Let's go and see if it checks out."

***

West Ocean Drive was easy to find. Laura parked the car alongside the very obvious site of Lighting The Way, a half-shell of a storefront that was covered in construction materials. Bags of sand and bricks were laying around it like dropped eggs, and scaffolding supported what remained of the structure. Some of it was still visibly blackened from the fire. The rest was new, brickwork going up to fill in the gaps that appeared to have been blown out by the flames.

"Excuse me?" Agent Won called out to a passing man. He was wearing a yellow hard hat and an orange reflective vest. Together with his slightly smarter clothing, compared to the other two men working on the site, Laura thought that Won had correctly guessed this to be the foreman.

The man wandered over, giving them an inquisitive look. "Yeah?"

"I was just wondering if you could tell us about this fire," Agent Won said. "It was a few months ago, right?"

"Yeah, pretty bad business," the foreman said, tilting his head to look up at the structure as if reassessing it for the first time. "One single candle was left on as a display item, and the whole place went up. We've been brought in to remodel and build it back up from what it was."

"It's going to be a candle store again?" Laura asked, surprised. She'd mostly expected to find an abandoned lot, if anything. It hadn't sounded in the news report as though Michael Noran had much intention of coming back.

"No, no," the foreman said, shaking his head. "We're building a restaurant. The lease for the store never got renewed after it was burned down, so I guess the owner thought it was time to move on. Get some more income in."

"So, there's no more candles?" Agent Won asked. "Or he just moved somewhere else?"

"No more candles. I don't know for sure, and you can ask him yourself, but I heard the guy who owned it lost everything in the fire. He didn't want to start all over again. Maybe couldn't. It's a real shame; tourists liked it a lot."

"Thanks," Agent Won said, letting the man go back to his work. He turned to Laura, his hands on his hips. "Sounds like we need to talk to the owner to get a better picture of what happened here."

Laura nodded. "I'm intrigued," she said. "The news report said it was a stray candle that started the whole blaze, and that guy just repeated it. But how would they know?"

"What do you mean?" Agent Won asked, frowning.

"Well, you have a whole store full of candles and other flammable items," Laura said, gesturing to the blackened arch above one of the empty windows. "When you go and look at it all later, how do you know that one of those candles started it? And even if you know there was no accelerant or other signs of arson, how do you know for sure that a candle was the original source? There would be no way to trace the fire to a single, individual candle."

"You think this could be the work of our pyromaniac?" Agent Won asked, his eyes lighting up.

"I wouldn't get too excited just yet," Laura said, studying the building one last time. "But maybe. Let's go talk to this Michael Noran and find out what he has to say about the whole situation."

CHAPTER SIXTEEN

Laura thought that it was good luck – or maybe not, given what they were investigating – that the owner of the candle store was still living in town. Despite losing everything in the blaze, Michael Noran had not moved on, and was still living in the same home he'd owned when he was working in his own store every day.

Laura let Agent Won approach the home first, going ahead to knock on the front door. It wasn't a cheap-looking property: the yard was beautifully manicured and sculpted, with rose bushes shaped just so and flowerbeds beneath them looking ripe for spring. The home itself was decently sized, a two-floor building with a portico around the entrance and a few solar panels on the roof. Given its position towards the beachfront and in a town like this, Laura had to assume it had cost a pretty penny.

The man who opened the door was the same one she had seen in the photographs accompanying the article: balding, a little overweight, but with dark beetling brows and a tall stature. "Hello?" he said, looking at them suspiciously as though he though they were about to sell him something. Maybe, given their dark suits, a religion.

"Michael Noran," Laura said, showing her badge. "We're with the FBI. We'd like to talk to you a bit about your store and the circumstances of it burning down, as well as a few events that have been happening around Pacific Cove recently. Can we come in?"

He looked affronted, right away. Like there was no way he wanted to let a couple of strangers into his home, and now that he knew they were FBI agents, he was even less interested. But that didn't mean he was going to have a choice. He spoke to them here, or at the precinct. Laura gave him an even look, until he seemed to get it.

"Okay," he said, at last, pulling back from the door. "Just… brush off your shoes before you come in, will you?"

Laura had to hold back a smirk as Agent Won obediently did as he was told, scuffing his feet across the welcome mat to dislodge any dirt. There was no reason for them not to do it. In fact, it was something she did automatically whenever she entered someone's home, because she wasn't rude and didn't like to leave them with a mess to clean up. But there was something about how Won just did as he was instructed that made her want to deliberately not do it at all. She made a perfunctory movement on the threshold and then stepped right through, following the figure of Michael Noran into a newly built sunroom.

Noran sat in a wicker chair there, letting it take his weight as he looked at them both. He had a guarded expression already, which meant he was not going to be easy to talk to necessarily. But that also buoyed Laura up a little. Those who wanted least to talk were often the ones with the most to hide.

"Can you tell us what happened to your store?" Laura asked, taking the initiative even as she and Agent Won both sunk down on a matching wicker sofa with a floral-patterned cushioned seat. "Lighting The Way, wasn't it?"

"I'd have thought you'd be able to get all of the details from the local fire department," Noran said sniffly. "They were the ones who did all the investigation."

"We can," Laura said, in a light tone that suggested they, indeed, would. "But I'd like to hear it from you. Your account, from the horse's mouth, so to speak."

If he had disliked their presence already, she could see that Noran liked being compared to a horse even less. His nostrils flared, a coincidence that Laura found highly amusing. He didn't even know he was making himself look even more like a horse by doing it. She was in a contrary mood to begin with thanks to all the confusion of this case, and there was nothing wrong in running with it when you had a suspect like this.

Because he was a suspect, given how cagey he was already behaving. And with a man like this, it would be easy to sting him enough that he blurted out something he wasn't supposed to. A death by a thousand cuts, resulting in him losing his temper and snapping out the truth.

"There's not much to say," Michael replied. "I owned a candle store, and we would often have a candle burning on display to show customers what they could expect. One night, I had an employee lock up and they forgot to blow out the candle before leaving. Somehow, it must have fallen over or something and the flame caught the display it was sitting on, and spread to the other candles, and pretty soon all my stock went up in flames along with the store itself."

"You've decided not to reopen?" Laura asked. "We just went by the site. It's apparently being remodeled as a restaurant now."

Michael nodded, looking down as if he was too sad to think about it. "I couldn't afford to start up again."

"Didn't your insurance pay out?" Laura asked.

Michael made a vague movement with his hand and his head, a kind of dismissal. "I didn't get enough to consider opening up again. The rebuilding alone was going to cost me a fortune. I had to give up my dream."

There was something about the way he was speaking that just didn't sit right with her. It wasn't just the way he so clearly didn't want them to be there. It was the way he spoke the words – almost like they were rehearsed. He'd spoken about losing his dream in the interview, too. The same words.

It was possible that he'd been asked about it so many times that he simply had stock answers ready to go, but...

"Did you feel any suspicion that your employee started the fire on purpose?" Laura asked. What she really wanted to know was whether Michael himself could have done something but asking that outright would only get his back up. Going after someone else instead could have better results. The thing she really wanted to analyze, anyway, was his reaction.

"It was an accident," Michael repeated, as if she was too stupid to understand what he was saying. "The fire department and the police both said so."

"I know they did," Laura said evenly. "I want to know what you thought about it. Did you ever have the feeling that the fire might not have been started by accident? Like maybe your employee enjoyed playing with fire?"

Michael snorted, shaking his head. "The insurance wouldn't have paid out if it wasn't an accident."

Two mentions of the insurance. Not much effort to protect the reputation of his employee. That was interesting.

Normally, Laura would expect a range of responses mostly hinged around the innocence of the employee. The owner might react with shock and talk about how good that employee was, how bad they'd felt since it happened. Or they might talk about how yes, it was possible, they had their own suspicions. They might even rant about how the person had been careless, but ultimately made a mistake. But Michael clearly didn't care about his employee's reputation.

It sounded more to Laura like he was trying to justify the insurance payout and ensure that no one looked into the possibility of taking it away from him.

"Where were you last night, in the late evening?" Laura asked, because if he didn't have an alibi there was a possibility that this needed to be taken further.

"What?" Michael blinked. "I was here."

"Alone?"

"With my wife."

Laura caught Agent Won looking at her and glanced his way. His expression was skeptical, and she felt the same. A wife was not exactly a reliable source for an alibi. A wife could reasonably be expected to lie in order to save her husband from prison. Especially if she assumed he was innocent, and this would all be blown out of proportion.

"And two nights ago – on Saturday?"

"I was here," Michael said, frowning. "Why?"

"Two nights before that?" Laura pressed.

Michael's expression cleared, but then clouded in an altogether different way. "This is about the murders," he said, obviously having put two and two together with the dates. "You're asking me for an alibi!"

"Yes, I am," Laura said. "So? Where were you, and can anyone else testify to that?"

"On Thursday I was out at the bar," Michael said.

"How late?"

He struggled. "I… Probably eight, or nine. I don't remember."

"Not late enough," Laura said. She was watching him closely. Something about his reaction, once again, struck her as not quite right. He was acting like he was on the back foot. Like he hadn't expected to be asked about this topic at all. He'd been all gung-ho and ready to defend himself – but not on this. It had thrown him for a loop. He was distracted. His eyes darted in all directions, and Laura noticed him wiping the palm of his hand discretely on his knee. He was sweating.

So, if he'd been expecting them to come and interrogate him on something else, what was it?

"Have you ever eaten at the Fresh Catch diner?" Agent Won asked, picking up the thread of the murders while Laura tried to get a handle on what Noran was hiding.

"Yes," he said. He was stammering slightly, casting nervous glances around. "Of course I have. Everyone has. It's one of the only local options."

"And have you ever ordered something or sat in at the Rise and Shine café?"

"Of course, I have!"

"How about getting gas at the gas station on Ocean View Boulevard?"

"Well – I mean – it's right on my way to work!"

Agent Won looked at Laura expectantly. She could see it in him: that eagerness, as always. He was waiting for her to arrest the guy, or at least give him permission to do so. But he was making a mistake. Laura could see there was something else going on here, something that Michael Noran didn't want them to find out about.

Laura got up, noticing how he practically jumped out of his seat when she did so. Like he was scared of something. Scared of what?

What didn't he want her to see or know?

"You mentioned your wife," Laura said. "Is she home at the moment?"

"No," Noran said, watching her hawklike, his gaze only briefly straying back to Agent Won as if he was trying to keep an eye on what they were both doing. His anxiety levels seemed to have shot up the moment she stood. "No, she's out at the store."

"Getting what?" Laura asked. She took a step experimentally to the side, saw sweat break out on Noran's brow, and took another.

"I... some supplies," Noran said. "You know, food and stuff. Where are you going?"

Laura had moved forward enough to see just down the hall into a part of the house they hadn't yet been shown. And what she saw made her want to smile, because now she knew she had him.

"I think the more accurate question is, where are you going?" she asked. "Since you have your suitcases already packed, I mean."

Noran went pale. "I'm going on vacation," he said. "There's no law against that."

"Vacation?" Laura repeated. "I haven't been on a vacation in months. Where are you headed?" She kept her tone conversational, even though she knew – and she knew that Noran knew – there was far more of a dangerous subtext to her question.

"Just for a quick trip," he said.

"You know that we can track travel records," Laura said, giving him an even look.

Noran quailed at that, looking away. "We're spending two weeks in Cancun."

"Two weeks," Laura said, whistling. "You ever had a two-week vacation, Agent Won?"

"Not since I was a kid," he said, scratching the back of his head. "We used to go back to Korea to visit my grandparents for a few weeks at a time."

"You were staying with family, though. That would have saved a lot." Laura looked at Noran. "Bet you're not staying with family, are you, Michael?"

"No," he said, sounding like it was the last thing in the world he wanted to admit.

"Must have cost you a pretty penny, then," Laura said. "Something in the region of, oh, say, an insurance payout?"

"It's not costing us all of it," Noran snapped. "I'm not that frivolous."

"Interesting," Laura said. "Agent Won, do you recall Mr. Noran here telling us that he didn't get enough of an insurance payout to restart his business?"

"I do," Agent Won nodded, playing along eagerly.

"And yet, he can afford a vacation," Laura said. "It's almost as if he's desperate to get out of the country for some reason. Mexico, didn't you say?"

Noran swallowed. "It's just a vacation," he said. "After the stress of the store burning down, we wanted to get away."

"Is that what happened?" Laura said. She put her hands on her hips, leaning towards him, unleashing a more menacing tone. "Or did you realize the FBI were getting closer to your trail and decided to book a vacation out of here so you would be able to disappear once you're over the border?"

"N-no!" Noran burst out, his face paler than ever and his eyes wide. "It's just a vacation, I swear!"

"Should I arrest him now?" Agent Won asked, clearly too excited about the prospect to play it cool any longer. "Or do you want the honors?"

"Oh, I think I'll take them," Laura said, because she wasn't actually ready to arrest him yet. She wanted to play for time. For stress. Make

Noran realize just how much trouble he was in, how much more he was going to be in if this wasn't stopped.

She had a feeling. She just needed him to confirm it himself.

"Please!" Noran said, holding up his hands in the universal gesture of innocence. "I didn't do anything to those girls – I didn't!"

"That's not what your face tells me, Michael," Laura said, taking out her handcuffs and holding them in front of herself like she was getting ready to snap them on him. "Your face tells me you're as guilty as sin."

"Not of this!" Noran said, sweating and breathing hard. He was sitting back in his chair, like the harder he sat down the less capable they would be of dragging him out of there, as if it would make a difference. "I didn't! I didn't hurt anyone! It was just... it was just a little fire!"

"Just a little fire," Laura repeated, narrowing her eyes at him. "What was, Michael?"

"The... the store," he said, beginning to wail. "I burned it down. I did. I admit it. I just wanted the insurance payout so I could retire and take my wife on vacation. I didn't want anyone to get hurt. No one did! It was just a harmless stunt, that's all, just something to get us out of the retail business – I didn't mean any harm by it!"

Laura took a breath, sighing it out. And there it was. The admission. She knew that he was telling the truth. She'd sensed it as soon as she'd spotted the parts of his story that didn't add up. The fact that he'd had an insurance payout and yet didn't want to try to rebuild his so-called dream, the over-rehearsed lines.

He was a criminal, yes. A fraud. But he wasn't a killer.

Which, while it did solve a crime, also left them right back at square one. No suspect. No lead they could follow.

And no idea how to stop the killer from striking again.

CHAPTER SEVENTEEN

Laura slumped in the driver's seat for a long moment, too tired to think about starting the engine. Out in front of their windshield, a silent cop show was playing out: Michael Noran ducking his head to get into the car with one of the local police as he was taken in for his part in the insurance fraud. To make Laura even more sure that he was innocent of the murders, his wife had shown up right before they took him in – and she was loudly protesting about how he was too unwell with his MS to sit in a police cell.

There was no way, apparently, he would have had the physical strength and speed needed to commit the murders, even if they had still had reason to suspect him.

He would be dealt with and processed by the Pacific Cove PD. No reason for Laura and Agent Won to involve themselves any further. He wasn't the person they were here for.

Which still left the nagging question: who was?

"Where do we go now?" Agent Won asked. He sounded just as weary and frustrated as she felt, but he was showing it a lot more. Getting surly. He didn't yet have the experience to preserve his poker face at a time like this.

Laura tapped the steering wheel thoughtfully, pretending that she was just watching them take Noran in and not experiencing a moment of existential despair. "We have to go back to the drawing board," she said. "Reassess everything we think we know and go back to the beginning. There might be something we've overlooked."

"There's nothing!" Agent Won said, gesturing in the air with a frustrated hand. "We've looked at everything. And what's with all these suspects not being right? It's so weird, it's like someone's playing us! Like we're being tricked – all of them seemed so obvious!"

Laura shot him a look. "You haven't done many cases," she said. It wasn't a question, since she already knew it was true. Even if he hadn't admitted it already, she would have known it by his attitude.

"So what?" Agent Won huffed.

"So, you don't know that this is what it's like," Laura said. "Endlessly tracking down the leads, from the most obvious to the least, despairing, thinking you're never going to get anywhere. Being so right, up until the moment you find out you're completely wrong. That's why it's so important for detectives to keep an open mind about their cases. Once you shut yourself in with tunnel vision and start twisting the facts to fit the conclusion you've already come to, you've lost the chance to solve the case. We won't know the full picture until we know the full picture. The way things look can be deceptive."

Agent Won sighed, though this time it sounded a little less petulant. "It's like this every single time?"

"More or less." Laura shot him a wry smile. "Still want to be an FBI agent?"

Agent Won caught her look and ended up smiling back. "I'm probably an idiot, but yeah."

"Well, you're in good company," Laura said, knowing she was probably the same. She sighed, settling more comfortably into the car seat. "Let's go back over what we know, start looking at the smaller threads that we haven't picked up yet. Like the candles, for example. We know they're sold across a wider area, but they must have been purchased here in town – it's too much of a coincidence, otherwise. I'll ask for a look at the sales records of Noran's candle store while they're going through his books, see if there's anyone who comes up time and time again for the kind of candle we're looking for. In the meantime, we can check out any other retailers in the area who stock the candles made at the factory."

"We have the list of stocks from them already," Won said, loading up something on his cell phone. "I think I remember there were only a few stores in town. Yeah, here we are – three stores. The general store, a souvenir store on Main Street, and what sounds like a kind of hippie incense place down by the water."

Laura nodded, starting the engine. "Alright, then," she said. "Let's go."

Pacific Cove was not a big town, and all three stores were set within a few blocks of one another. As she drove towards the first, Laura couldn't help thinking about her visions again, trying to go over them one more time. The flames snuffed out, leaving only smoke trailing in their wake. What did it mean? She was at least sure that it was connected to their killer, but... how?

If only she could be sure that it was a totally useless vision, one of those that came out of nowhere and had no bearing on any case, then she would be able to stop thinking about it and move on. But as it was,

Laura couldn't dismiss it. Just in case there was something she needed to know, something she hadn't yet worked out, she needed to keep turning it over in her head.

"I think this is it," Won said, gesturing ahead. There was a small space for parking on the side of the road outside the store, and Laura slid the car into it before unbuckling her seatbelt. Won was out of the car before she was, bounding towards the store with that endless enthusiasm of his. There were some advantages to having a rookie agent around, after all, Laura thought as she followed him. Right now, she had no enthusiasm left, and she was starting to run out of any kind of energy.

He stepped inside the store first and went right up to the counter, walking down an aisle that stocked such diverse things as hammers and nails, cell phone cases, dog toys, and fishing magazines. There was an older man behind the counter in a flannel shirt, and he greeted them with the kind of confidence that made Laura feel he was almost certainly the owner.

"Hi, I'm Special Agent Eric Won," he said, showing his badge. "I'm here with my partner, Special Agent Laura Frost, just investigating the murders that you've been having here in Pacific Cove. I wondered if you could tell us about any customers you've had in here buying candles?"

"Candles?" the man behind the counter grunted, though not in an unfriendly way. "I don't know. We sell a few, not a huge amount."

"You stock them from the local factory, isn't that right?" Eric said. Laura stayed back, letting him handle things. With one ear on the conversation in case something did come up, she could use the rest of her attention to think about the problem they had to solve. About how to track down the killer in other ways, in case this angle – local candle sales – didn't work out.

"Sure," the man said, gesturing to the left. There was a display of candles there, Laura saw. She walked over, picking up one of the thicker models that matched the kind the killer was using. "We don't take too many. Just a few every month. They sell, but not as much as most of our other stock."

"Can you recall any particular resident who has bought several?" Eric asked. "It doesn't have to be all in one transaction. Maybe there's someone who comes in and buys them over and again?"

"No," the store owner said, shaking his head slowly side to side. A frown had settled between his black brows, like he was thinking hard.

"I can't think of anyone who comes back often. Maybe a couple of the older ladies who like to buy a candle for their husbands' birthdays, light them in remembrance."

"What about over the last couple of weeks?" Eric persisted. "Have you sold any at all? Particularly of the type my partner is holding?"

The owner shook his head again. "Maybe. Sorry. I think one or two, perhaps. It's not often we sell those ones. I can look up the records, but as far as I recall, it's just a couple of the widows, like I mentioned."

"Thanks," Eric sighed, scratching a hand through the hair at his temple. "If you could get those records, just in case."

Laura sighed as the owner went into the back, shaking her head. "I have a feeling we're not going to get a lot of success with this route," she said, feeling the weight of truth in the words.

"Shouldn't we stay positive?" Eric replied, lifting an eyebrow, and Laura only shot him a tired a look.

***

"Well, I was right," Laura said, without any real sense of satisfaction. The other two stores in town held a similar story. Very few candles sold, and when they were, it was often to the older members of the population. While Laura couldn't rule out one of them having a relative who requisitioned the candles for their own use, she did find it unlikely to imagine that it was a little old lady cutting the throats of these girls and then moving their bodies.

Which meant they were no closer to getting anywhere than they had been before.

"We haven't had any lunch yet," Eric complained, as they walked out of the last place – the hippie incense place, as he'd called it, which left Laura feeling slightly unwell from the thick wreaths of scented smoke that hung in the air there. "I can't think on an empty stomach."

Laura checked her watch with a growing sense of despair. She hadn't even thought about food, but now that he'd mentioned it… it was already past two in the afternoon, which meant lunchtime had come and gone.

"Fast food only," Laura cautioned him. "We need something we can eat on the move. We haven't got time to sit down for a meal with a plate."

"We haven't got any leads to follow," Eric groused. "I don't see why we can't sit down for five minutes."

"Because we're running out of time again," Laura told him. "He's going to claim another victim soon. Maybe tomorrow. But maybe – and my suspicion is, more likely – tonight."

"Why would he change his MO?" Eric asked. "It's always been two days between."

"Because this is a small town, and we've been talking to a lot of people." Laura rubbed her forehead, trying to cut off the headache that was trying to form there. Not a vision headache – just the normal kind, from the lack of sleep and the stress of the case. "I have no doubt now that he knows, whoever he is, that the FBI are in town. He knows we're coming for him. And from what I know of all the killers I've tried to track down in the past, he'll want to keep going and take as many victims as he can before he gets caught. Which means escalating, stepping up the pace – and that could mean someone is in danger tonight."

Eric sighed, a little melodramatically. "There's a burger joint up on the corner," he said. "I saw it when we passed through earlier. It has a to-go window. We'd better get everything wrapped up."

Laura was about to admonish him for not taking things seriously, but then she caught a look at his face. He looked tired, too, and stressed out. Like he was having a hard time coping with the pressure of the case. She guessed that, when she thought about it, being hungry on top of all that was probably an unpleasant feeling. She bit her tongue, leaving him be.

Laura started the car back up, even though it was beginning to feel stupid to drive around a town of this size. Of course, they need to be able to move quickly if they had a lead to chase down, but right now it felt like they were just burning fossil fuels for no results. All they were running into were dead ends.

Maybe Eric was right. A greasy takeout burger might give Laura's brain a bit of fuel and put her in the right frame of mind to see what she was missing.

"What do you want?" Eric asked, as they pulled up alongside the takeout window.

Laura shrugged. She hadn't even had the headspace to look at the menu they were driving by. "Whatever you're having," she said.

Eric leaned across her towards the teenager behind the window, rattling out an order that Laura also did not pay attention to. She was thinking about the time. It was late enough to have lunch, and there was a six-hour flight required before she would be back at home.

It was looking more and more like it was time to admit defeat and text Chris.

She sighed at the thought, a wave of frustration coming over her. There were so many reasons to get this case done fast, and yet she didn't seem to be able to achieve it for any of them.

"Ma'am?" the teen said, and Laura snapped to attention enough to realize that she was holding out a brown paper bag towards her, emblazoned with the logo of the fast-food place. Laura took it and handed it off directly to Eric, then accepted a couple of coffees in a cardboard tray and passed those across as well. She pulled out of the to-go lane, back out onto the road.

"Where are we going?" she asked. She meant to park and eat, but she also recognized the irony in the question. It was what Eric had been asking her about the case for the last few days.

"Over by the shore?" Eric suggested. "There's a lookout point not far from here I spotted last night, thought it might be a nice spot in the daytime."

Laura followed his directions and they pulled up, staring out at the sea. It was quiet, barely stirring in the breeze. It could have been a perfect summer's day, given the blue, clear sky and the stillness of the waves, except for the wintry cold. Laura accepted the coffee back gratefully and took a sip, not minding the slight burn on her tongue that she received for starting it too soon. The caffeine was needed badly enough to override the pain.

"Here," Eric said, nudging her to take a paper-wrapped burger from his hands. She did so, accidentally brushing her hand across his as she took it and feeling a stab of pain.

Damnit.

Now she was probably going to find out more about Agent Won than she —

She was looking into the car, watching herself, as if she was floating outside the windshield. There she was with a burger in one hand, half-unwrapped, a few bites taken out of it. And there was Agent Won next to her, having just gleefully taken the burger out of the wrapper completely, enjoying the last few bites of an overstuffed bun filled with just about every topping the fast-food joint had to offer.

He took a giant bite and the bright yellow blob of mustard squeezed out of the back of the bun, falling right down onto his white shirt. He exclaimed in dismay, grabbing a napkin and swiping at it, but it was no use. That bright yellow stain was there to stay.

Laura blinked, looking down at the burger in her hand. Well, that was something. Her visions *were* still working. It was just that the ones she was getting in relation to the case weren't getting her anywhere.

"You alright?" Eric asked, his tone one of genuine concern. He'd already taken the first bite of his burger, keeping it wrapped halfway for now.

"Yes," Laura said, shaking it off. "I just realized I need to send someone a message. Be careful with these burgers – looks like there's a lot of sauce in them."

"You haven't even opened yours yet," Eric said, frowning a little.

She nodded her head towards him. "I don't need to. I can see yours." She opened the packaging with one hand and then grabbed her cell phone as she took the first bite, scrolling to her most recent conversation with Chris and opening it.

Hey, sorry. I'm still on the case out here. I'm not going to be able to make it back to D.C. in time for tonight. I have to cancel. Maybe we can do another night?

She felt a gnawing ache in her stomach as she sent the text, the kind of nervous reaction she always had when she got the feeling that she was letting someone down. It was an awful feeling. She waited for his response, trying not to see the fact that there were still so many messages Nate had not bothered to reply to. At this point, she wouldn't be surprised if he had simply blocked her number. And if he had, she had no way of getting in contact with him save walking right up to his door – which would probably not do her any favors, either.

Her phone buzzed, and she opened the message hastily to read it. It was from Chris, of course, and while she was glad to hear back from him, she was also annoyed at the way her heart lurched with disappointment with every message or call that wasn't from Nate.

Sorry to hear that! Hope you get it wrapped up soon. I can't make the rest of this week – I'm on shift and then I've got a meeting with Amy's teachers on Friday to see how she's settling in. Playdate this weekend still good?

Laura sighed to herself as she sent back a confirmation for the weekend. A playdate was all well and good, but it was for the girls – not their respective guardians. It was a time for tea parties and dolls and watching inane children's shows, not having eyes meet over candlelit dinners. Between the fact that they had two of the busiest jobs Laura could imagine – agent and doctor – and their lives as parents, she was starting to wonder if this thing was doomed before they even started it. When would they even get a chance to see one another?

"I wish we would just get something that panned out," Eric grumbled. It came so out of the blue, Laura almost jumped.

"We'll get something eventually," she said. It was the kind of thing she told herself for reassurance, even though it didn't always make her feel better. "We have to. We're not letting him slip away."

"What if it's too late?" Eric said, frustration evident in his voice. "We've already let one girl die on our watch. I really wanted to do well on this first one."

"Don't worry," Laura said, though she wasn't exactly feeling calm about it herself. "We'll get him. We just have to keep thinking. Keep seeing what we haven't seen yet, figuring it out."

And the same applied, she reminded herself, to both Nate and Chris. It felt like one new flame in her life was being lit, and she didn't want it to be extinguished before she ever got the chance to find out how brightly it would burn. They would figure something out.

Extinguished...

Laura's mind shot forward, going over that vision again. Flames being extinguished. What if they were seeing everything the wrong way?

"I have a new theory," she said, working it out even as she spoke out loud. "We've been thinking that the killer uses candles because he's obsessed with flames. But what if it's the other way around? What if it's the fact of the candle being snuffed out that is the point?"

Eric spoke around a mouthful of burger. "But wouldn't that mean his method is wrong? He doesn't get to blow the candle out. Whoever finds the body does."

"It's still symbolic," Laura said, hesitating then rushing on as her mind worked this new angle. "In fact, it might be even *more* symbolic for it. This idea of the final resting place of the victim, their discovery and then their light going out forever once someone other than the killer knows that they're gone."

"I don't get it," Eric said, shrugging. "Sorry."

"Well, think about it," Laura said. "Candles are symbolic. They always have been. They represent light against the darkness. They have religious overtones, used in ceremonies even today. Not because we need them – we have electricity now. Because of how symbolic they are. And we even use it as a metaphor – we talk about a candle being blown out to symbolize the end of something, even a life."

Eric shrugged again. "Sounds like something my English teacher would say," he said. "I don't know if the killer is that deep." He took the last half of his burger out of the wrapper and put it to his mouth with some relish, taking a massive bite.

A dollop of mustard fell neatly out of the back and splattered on his shirt, making him cry out in dismay.

"Damnit!" he said, dabbing at it with a napkin. Laura didn't need to look to see that that yellow stain was going to be there for the foreseeable future.

"I did tell you to be careful," she said mildly. It wasn't her fault if people ignored her warnings. It wasn't as though she could force them to pay attention.

"I should change this shirt," Eric said, grabbing the wrapper to hold it under the last few bites of his burger as he wolfed it down. "I have a spare clean one at the motel."

"No can do," Laura said. "You'll just have to do up your jacket if it bothers you. We've got to get to the bottom of this – figure out what the candles mean and why the killer is using them. Once we know that, we might just know him."

Eric sighed. "Look, no offense, but that just sounds like psychobabble to me," he said. "I'm good at investigating, not profiling. If that's your thing, whatever, but I'd rather follow real leads. I still think we're onto something with the whole firebug thing. I want to keep looking into that."

Laura could have pulled rank on him then and there, told him to shut up and pay attention. That she was the senior officer and he had to do as he was told. But on the other hand, even though she had warmed to him a little, she knew she was better off on her own. Without the distraction. She didn't need to be anyone's babysitter. And it was almost always better to have two agents pursuing two theories, rather than getting tunnel vision on one.

"Then do it on your own," she said.

"Cool," he said, and then, "Can you drop me off at the motel?"

CHAPTER EIGHTEEN

He watched her through the glass, pretending he was looking at the printouts advertising all the local homes for sale in the window. There were some nice ones, at least, that he might have lingered on if he really was in the market for a new home.

Not that he'd had to cultivate the impression that he was. She, Cherry, was admin assistant here in the real estate office, so he always knew that he could see her if he wanted to. He just had to drop by and look in the window. He could even go inside if he wanted to be nearer to her. But there was no need.

After all, he didn't know her from the work that she did. He hadn't had any reason to visit this office before, and so if it had been from that, they never would have met. No, Cherry was someone he knew from his own line of work, unlike the other girls. Their connection had started in a completely different way. She'd been the one to come to him.

That made her special, it really did. They were all special in their own different ways, but he loved the fact that Cherry was someone he knew from work. He wasn't just a customer to her like he was to the others. Actually, if anything, it was the other way around.

Not that Cherry could ever be described as 'just' anything. That would have been an understatement of her value to the highest degree.

Of course, it wasn't like he ever really thought she'd noticed him. He wasn't stupid enough to have those kinds of fantasies. He knew what he was, and he knew what she was. So far out of his league. She would never normally have given him the time of day, and if she glanced up now and saw him looking in, he reckoned she might not even recognize him.

She stood to move across the office with some files, and he admired the smart way she walked, the way she swayed from side to side in her heels. They did have a connection, even if she wasn't as aware of it as he was. It was there. And soon, he was going to make sure that that connection was complete.

He moved on from the window, judging that he had probably spent enough time standing there. Any longer, and people might start to get suspicious. He couldn't risk that, not now.

People were looking at each other these days. Wondering. They knew that there was a killer among their ranks, and they all wanted to be the one to figure out who. Either for protection, or for glory. He wasn't going to let that happen by doing something stupid and suspicious that would get fingers pointed in his direction – not when it was so easy to slip under the radar and just go on as he always had.

And it wasn't just the civilians. He moved down Main Street and noticed the police officer walking along in uniform, hands at his sides, surveying everyone with a casual yet alert manner. There were more and more of them out on the streets the last few days, it seemed. Patrols had become more regular. He'd seen the same cop car drive by at least three times since he started his afternoon stroll. They were just going around and around, desperate to catch any hint of a clue.

He was going to have to be extra careful tonight. Taking a day out of his schedule would confuse them at least a little, he hoped. If he waited until tomorrow, everyone would be so on edge and nervous that he would have very little chance of doing what he needed to do. At least, without getting caught.

And if he got caught halfway through? Well, that was even worse. To start without finishing would make a mockery of the whole thing.

He mentally rehearsed his plans, trying to test them for any points of weakness. It was imperative that he finish. Cherry didn't know him yet, but she would soon – so soon. And given how special he was, he wasn't going to let anything interrupt him before that happened.

He walked onwards down the street, feeling the budding excitement of another connection ready to be made. Tonight was going to be special.

Tonight, Cherry was going to connect with him in ways she couldn't even possibly imagine right now.

CHAPTER NINETEEN

Back at the precinct, Laura settled down in front of the desk she had been given and loaded up the computer, almost rolling her eyes at how slow it was. Why did it always seem like local police departments had the oldest, least functioning equipment in the entire world? At least in a backwater like this she had expected it; but then again, given the wealth of the town itself, it was still disappointing.

She started in a very simple way: she searched for 'candles,' and started reading the information that came up.

It quickly became apparent that there were a lot of rabbit holes that this research could take her down. She wasn't entirely surprised: like she'd said to Eric, candles had a lot of meaning to them. They'd been used for so long as the only means of illumination, meaning that they had a practical history as well as all of the layers of symbolism that had fallen on them over the centuries. Unpicking that wasn't going to be easy, particularly as she had no idea whether the killer was suffering from some kind of psychosis or reading them the way that they had always been read.

She started down a pathway that was somewhat interesting: the use of candles in ritual sacrifice. Almost any kind of so-called 'demonic rite' or Satanic ritual had the use of candles incorporated in some way. Sometimes they were blood-red or coal-black, and other times had to give off a particular scent. Sometimes, though, plain white candles of the kind used in church would be just fine. Of course, most of the research she found on the subject was heavily wrapped into pop culture and fiction. There was no such thing as real Satanism, at least not in the way the media sometimes portrayed it.

That didn't mean it couldn't count. There were killers in the past who had been inspired by movies or by books to commit their murders. At least, the method in which they committed them. Laura had come across enough killers to not believe in the story that violent movies and video games could create violent people. It was the violent people in the first place who were drawn to that kind of thing. People who either didn't develop a moral code to understand that killing or hurting others was wrong – or understood it and enjoyed it for precisely that reason.

114

This was the problem she was dealing with, the thorny briars she had to cut through: did the killer believe in what he'd been told, or was he capable of distinguishing the difference between fact and fiction? Was he perfectly rational and logical and yet also a killer, or was he suffering from psychosis? And without knowing more about his motivation, how could she even tell?

Laura doubled down, emerging from her rabbit hole about sacrifice and going back to the more pure and factual roots of candle use. They had been used to light the way for centuries – the same thought that had occurred to her earlier. But today? The largest use of candles was in religious ceremonies, most notably in churches of various Christian denominations.

Laura rubbed her lower lip, thinking. The dominant religion of the population around here would match that, of course, and she had seen a couple of churches around town as they were driving. In a cultural sense, Caucasians living in the US were far more likely to be influenced by Christian symbology than by that of any other religion, since most of them would have grown up learning about or even being raised in that faith. It stood to reason, then, that anything done by a killer living locally was most likely to be influenced in some way by that symbology.

Unless their killer was a minority, of course, which would throw everything off. But killers, especially the kind who earned the moniker 'serial,' were usually white men. If she was following the statistics, she should logically focus on this area of research.

Laura checked her phone, seeing no messages from anyone – no reply from Chris, no call back from Nate, no indication of what Eric was up to out there. She tried not to worry about any of it. She had to get on with this, now, and get back home so at least one of her worries would be taken care of. Three more days and she needed to be picking up Lacey for another weekend together. Christ. Her life seemed to be a rush these days, always a dead sprint from one thing to the other, always worried she wouldn't make it in time.

"Religion," Laura muttered under her breath, trying to keep herself on track. What did candles mean in religion, especially in connection with death? She thought about people filing into a church, lighting a candle in prayer. They were a way to send a message to God, to have your prayer heard.

She thought, too, about a memorial service. An image came to her head, probably something she'd seen on television or in a movie, of a

115

misty scene, mourners around a coffin. A large-printed portrait of the deceased propped up in front of it and surrounded by white flowers. All around and among the scene, white candles burning, fat bodies and strong flames. Memorial.

Didn't that kind of feel like what the killer was doing? The way the women were found, it was almost as though their hands were crossed over their chests in prayer. Like they were posing for that open coffin service.

She had something here, she thought. They were placed down carefully, almost reverentially, and then a candle was lit for them. A candle that would burn brightly in the night and lead to their discovery. There was something, now that she connected the thought, about the funeral service in it.

So, was that it? Memorial? A way for him to remember them?

She glanced out of the window at the slowly darkening sky, realizing that it was getting on for the evening now. She didn't have long to get this figured out. She would go to each of the churches in town, she thought, speak to the staff there, try to get a fix on –

"Agent Frost!"

Laura turned her head sharply to see Eric entering the room, a wide grin plastered on his face. He was slightly out of breath, his hair a little damp around the temples, as though he'd recently engaged in some kind of exertion. And behind him, he was dragging a young man in handcuffs – a young man with a wide-eyed look and a conspicuously muddy rip in his blue jeans.

"Agent Won?" she responded, frowning.

"I have our killer!" he exclaimed triumphantly, his chest practically swelling up as he said it.

Laura blinked.

"Excuse me?" she said, getting up from the desk with a rattle, not minding the fact that she'd bumped her thigh into it as she stood with haste. She started to rush towards him, as did most of the other few cops in the room.

"Let's get him processed," Eric said, turning to one of the cops who always seemed to be at the precinct – a desk sergeant who was perfectly placed to go through the paperwork. "I want to start questioning as soon as possible." Handing the kid over, he stood with his hands on his hips in a self-satisfied pose as he watched a cabal of the locals taking him over to a relevant desk.

Laura grabbed his outstretched elbow and steered him away quickly, pulling him to the furthest side of the room. It wasn't as far as she would have liked, but in a precinct of this size, that couldn't exactly be helped.

"What's going on?" she hissed at him, trying not to be overheard by anyone else.

"I found him," Eric said, with that same self-satisfied air. He was clearly riding high, impressed with himself and on top of the world. "Our killer. It's him."

Laura shook her head impatiently, feeling like she needed a diagram of some kind at this point to figure out exactly what he was thinking. "Do you care to explain any of this to me?"

"Sure," Eric said, breezily, clearly not picking up on her annoyance. "I found him while going through the records of local crimes, like we said. He's a bit of a petty criminal with a small record, but it didn't show up on our first search because of his age. He's only twenty-one, and the majority of his crimes happened before he was eighteen, so they were juvenile records."

Laura nodded; she was with him so far. At least, she understood. It might have been nice if she'd literally been *with* him, given that he'd seemingly acted on all this discovery without his senior agent present. "And what were those records?"

"Vandalism, for the most part," Eric said. "He was known for setting small fires. It only came up because I was talking with Detective Waters, and he remembered this little kid that got in trouble for setting a fire in the school gym. Turns out it wasn't his first or his last offense."

"Okay," Laura said slowly. "And his connection to our victims?"

"He was at school with Cici Powers," Eric said, his grin only getting wider. He really was impressed with himself on this one. "And as for the other two, he was a frequent customer at both the diner and the coffee shop. I know we pointed out already that a lot of the locals are, but given his age, he'd be more likely to interact with them on a closer level."

Laura glanced across the other side of the room, to where this suspect was still talking to the other cops. She saw one of them push a fingerprint pad towards him. "Who is this kid?"

"Jonas Mendez," Eric supplied readily. "He was at home when we went and knocked on the door. He seemed surprised to see us at first, and everything was fine. But when I tried to arrest him, that's when he ran."

"And fell," Laura said, raising an eyebrow at that muddy tear in his pants.

"Yeah, he tripped over himself," Eric said with a chuckle. "Can you believe that? Anyway, it wasn't hard to bring him in."

"What has he said so far?" Laura asked, wishing she wasn't playing catchup. She trusted her own instincts far more than anyone else's. If she had seen things first-hand, she could make much better judgement calls about them.

"He just babbled some things about being innocent and having no idea why we were taking him in," Eric shrugged. "Just like you'd expect a murderer to say, really."

"Alright," Laura said, glancing over. The local cops were finishing up processing the kid's details. "I need you to show me everything you have on him right away – records, proof of interaction, all of it. Then I'll go and talk to him."

Eric frowned slightly. "You mean, we'll go talk to him, right?"

"No," Laura said. "I mean, me. You've already gone against what we agreed by going ahead and arresting someone on your own instead of calling me first. You know I'm the senior agent. We should have discussed this beforehand."

"Why?" Eric asked, his facing dropping. He looked like a kid getting told off himself. "I could tell it was him. I thought you'd want me to use my initiative."

"There's such a thing as strategy, Agent Won," Laura said. "For example, the kind of strategy that doesn't end up with our suspect getting injured in the case, leaving us open to criticism, if we can help it."

Agent Won made a little movement with his mouth as if he was going to argue back, but then clamped it shut and led her over to the computer. There on the screen was everything he had: the juvenile arrest records, the school records, everything he had on Jonas Mendez.

Which, yes, was a little suspicious. He was known for starting small fires. But none of them had any connection to candles, there was no sign of violence in his past, and Laura couldn't see that there was much in it besides a teenager acting out for attention.

She glanced at Eric, at how he stood with his hands on his hips, waiting for her to come around to his side. He looked supremely confident. And, yes, on the surface of it, there was a lot here to be suspicious of.

But like she'd told him before, he just didn't have the experience. He wasn't used to profiling, to understanding the difference between a petty criminal and a killer. To seeing the red flags in someone's past, the same things that tended to come up time and time again. And while he might have found a number of coincidental overlaps in Mendez's history, he'd forgotten something important: any real indication of motive.

On top of that, he simply couldn't read people yet. Laura could. And she couldn't read what he wanted her to in this kid.

Were there any more ways the universe could point out to her that working with Eric was nothing, nothing at all, like working with Nate? She wished he was there right now. They might have argued, gone in separate directions – but he never would have made a stupid arrest like this and wasted time.

"Stay here," she sighed, rubbing a hand across her forehead crossly. "I'll be back in a few minutes."

Because, honestly, she couldn't even see this needing to take that long.

CHAPTER TWENTY

Laura walked to the interview room – which was not exactly far away, given how small the precinct was. She'd even been able to watch the locals walking Mendez over to it, which was why she had no need to ask where he was. She walked in and sat down in front of the kid, who looked downright awful: sweating, pale, wide-eyed, and jumpy. He looked at her with huge brown eyes under a head of curly hair, like a puppy begging not to be kicked.

"Jonas Mendez," Laura said, figuring it was best to jump right in. "Where were you yesterday evening?"

"At the skate park down by the beach," Jonas said, right away. "With my friends. I didn't do nothing. I swear I didn't. I don't know what this is all about – that crazy guy just tackled me!"

"Alright," Laura said, holding up a soothing hand to interrupt his babbling. She took a piece of paper out of the file she'd carried in – the file of his own printed records – and turned it over to the blank space on the back. She pushed it across the table to him along with her pen. "Write down the names of your friends, so we can check up with them and confirm what times you were there."

"It was all evening!" Jonas said. "I swear. I went there right after school, and we hung out until past midnight."

"School?" Laura frowned. "Your record says you're twenty-one."

"I'm doing classes at the community college in the next town over," Mendez explained. "I dropped out, but I went back."

That made sense. Laura nodded. "Do you want to tell me about the fires?"

Mendez looked at his hands. He almost looked tearful. Like he was ashamed of what he was about to say. "I just…"

"Yes?" Laura prompted. She could see the kid wasn't going to talk unless he was pushed.

"My mom had cancer," he said, at last. "A few years ago. She didn't make it. And I was just really… I just wanted to do something. I wanted to, like. I don't know. Burn the world. But not really. I was just acting out. It wasn't fair and I wanted to do something that wasn't fair. And it was stupid, and I got in a lot of trouble, and I don't do that

120

anymore. But people around here don't forget, and they still bring it up all the time."

Laura studied him. It had come out in such a rush. All of that information at once, and it didn't feel rehearsed or scripted to her. It felt like a kid who was scared and trying to express why he'd done something that people were never going to let him forget. Exactly what he said he was.

And he had an alibi.

"What about Saturday night?" Laura asked, just to be thorough.

"I work the night shift at the mall outside of town," he said. "I was with the other guy on shift all night. We hung out in the security hut and played cards."

That clinched it. All they had to do was verify both nights, and he was completely off the hook. He might have been able to find a friend to lie for him, or even one who was too high or drunk to remember him leaving but being at work all night was something else.

"Write down those names," Laura said. "Your friends, and your coworker as well. Someone will be by in a minute to collect them all from you. Don't lie or make something up, or you'll be in a lot more trouble than you've ever been in, got it?"

Mendez nodded miserably, snatching the pen up quickly and starting to scratch out a list of names as though his life depended on it.

Laura walked out and back into the main area of the precinct, where she could see Agent Won sitting on the side of the desk, surrounded by a few officers like before. They were all grinning and talking, and she saw one of them slap him on the side of the arm as she approached. Congratulating him. They all thought the case was solved.

"Right," she said, walking up to them and grabbing their attention quickly with the loud word. "You, I need you to go in there and take the list of names Mendez is writing down. You're going to follow up with each of them and see what they say about where he was last night, make sure his alibi stacks up. And you, you're going to release him." She pointed at two of the cops at random – Mandy, she thought, and Frank, though she still wasn't clear exactly on who was who.

"What?" Agent Won gaped, staring at her. "But he's our suspect!"

"Did you not hear me say alibi?" Laura half-growled. "The poor kid is terrified, and he obviously has nothing to do with this case."

Agent Won shot her a furious look. The two cops Laura had given instructions to quickly shuffled away, like they didn't want to hang around to hear any more. The third shot an anxious look around and then scuttled to a nearby desk. A wise choice, Laura thought.

"Can I talk to you outside?" Agent Won asked stiffly, standing up from the desk and buttoning up his suit jacket.

Laura sighed and rolled her eyes, but she led him out of the precinct all the same. It was darkening outside, almost completely night, the last traces of the sun's rays lingering just at the horizon. It was too late for this kind of thing. They had another death potentially on their hands tonight, and he wanted to act like a child. To sulk.

Laura was going to have to nip this in the bud, once and for all.

"Why did you do that?" Agent Won hissed, now that they were alone, outside in front of the precinct with the parking lot ahead of them. "Why did you have to show me up in front of them?"

"Show you up?" Laura scoffed. "This isn't high school, and I'm not your mother. You were wrong. This kid has an alibi − and if you'd taken more than a moment to talk to him rather than sitting around congratulating yourself, you'd have known that."

"I know it's not high school!" Agent Won blew up, his hair falling out of its neat style as he shook his head angrily. "You undermined me in front of them! We're supposed to be leading this investigation, and you made me look like some stupid kid!"

Laura pointed a finger towards his chest, getting closer to him than she needed to. The frustration, the anger at having to give up her plans, at having to find another body, at not solving what should have been a simpler case than this was getting under her skin. And Agent Won, who was not Nate and never would be Nate, was already right in the firing line. Getting in her face had been a mistake. Now, she was going to get in his.

"*I* am supposed to be leading this investigation," Laura snapped. "*You* are supposed to be following my lead and doing as you're told. You have no experience with this kind of case, you have no gut instinct, no investigative skills to speak of. You're supposed to be learning from me, and you're trying to take over as though you know exactly what you're doing. Well, you don't!"

"I have investigative skills!" Agent Won retorted, screwing his face up in anger. "I found that lead and brought him in! And I've been helping this whole time − you just don't ever want to listen to me!"

"You brought in a suspect who was in a public place at the time of the last murder with a group of his friends," Laura told him. "You want people to listen to you? That's called respect, and you have to earn it.

You shut up, you pay attention, and you listen to the people who actually know what they're doing. You're eager, and that's good – but you let your head and your excitement get away from you, and that's when you screw up!"

"So, I brought in a guy who turned out not to be the one – so what?" Agent Won said, folding his arms over his chest. "At least I'm *doing* something!"

"So, we just both wasted a hell of a lot of time looking in the wrong direction," Laura told him. "So, all the local cops were just standing around talk to you and patting you on the back instead of continuing to work the case. *So,* our killer is out there right now probably taking his next victim – and we needed all of that time you just wasted to catch him and stop him. *That's* so what!"

Agent Won blanched, shaking his head. "You can't blame me for the killer striking again," he said.

"Then who do I blame, Special Agent Won?" Laura asked, using his full title for effect. "We are here because the local police needed help. Because the people of this town needed help. It is our *job* to make sure that this killer gets caught and put away behind bars before he does any more damage. So, yes, I am going to blame you. And I am going to blame myself. Because no one else is going to solve this if we don't – do you understand that?"

"But," Agent Won said – but he couldn't seem to think of anything else to follow up the word, and his voice was faltering, dropping in volume and ire.

"Stop being so overzealous about every single lead we come across, or no one's ever going to take you seriously," Laura snapped. "Listen to your superiors and learn a few things before you start acting like you're God's gift to the FBI. And for God's sake, get off your high horse. You screwed up. Own it. And then get back to goddamn work, or you're going to be responsible for the death of another young woman!"

Agent Won seemed to struggle for words for a moment – and then he spat one out, seemingly at random. "Whatever," he said, like he was still a teenager, and then he pushed past Laura and stalked off back into the precinct.

Laura looked up into the sky, took a very deep breath, and counted to ten.

She rubbed her forehead, trying to calm down. This kid – he was a mess. Nowhere near ready for this kind of field work. What the hell had

Chief Rondelle been thinking, assigning him with her? Was he just hoping to distract and irritate her enough that she would stop calling him about Nate? Because if so, the tactic wasn't working. All this was doing was making her see just how good she'd had it over the past few years, to be assigned with a partner whose skill and demeanor matched hers beautifully.

There wasn't enough time left in the day to worry about Agent Won and his little hissy fit. She had to leave him behind. He'd chosen not to stick around and hear what the next step in the investigation was, and she was done holding his hand. She had to get moving and keep going until she brought the killer down.

What she'd said hadn't been a lie. Even right now, the killer could be out there, preparing to strike. Laura walked to the rental car in the parking lot, getting inside and firing up the GPS. It was time to go look into the local churches – and see if anyone there could shed any light on an unhealthy obsession with memorials or the use of candles for the dead.

CHAPTER TWENTY ONE

Laura pulled up outside the largest church in Pacific Cove, both by actual size and by congregation, as far as her research had suggested. She ducked her head, looking through the car window for a sign of life. There was light, she thought, shining through the stained-glass windows towards the back of the building. Someone must have been in there.

Laura got out of the car, holding her breath against the blast of cold that hit her. The night had fallen in earnest now, bringing with it even lower temperatures than the day. She tried not to think about a woman laying out there somewhere on the cold ground, her life bleeding away from a hole in her neck. Because if she thought about it too hard, Laura feared she was going to give in to absolute despair. And maybe there was still time. Yes, it was dark now – but it was winter. If the killer truly wanted to wait until night instead of evening, maybe she had an hour or two, some desperate small window to get this done.

She approached the massive entrance doors of the church and pushed; to her surprise, they opened easily and without much pressure. Stepping inside, she immediately saw the source of the light she had seen from outside. Candles – dozens of them – all set up together in front of the altar on a long, low framework designed for the purpose. Memorial candles.

Laura approached them, feeling hushed as she always did in a church environment, like she needed to watch her step, in case her shoes were too loud. The rest of the church seemed empty, even though that meant the candles were unattended – strange, Laura thought, and bad practice in a town where a candle store had burned down so recently. She crossed right down the aisle between the empty pews until she was standing in front of the candles, looking into their flames.

Into flames that seemed so familiar. A pattern that seemed engraved in her memory.

And now she knew. The flames – these were the same ones she had seen in her vision. The candles, too, were the same kind that were placed with the bodies. A few different kinds, which explained something about why those on the bodies had shown slight

125

differentiations in size and thickness. To one side, Laura spotted a long, thin device with a kind of cup on one end: an old-fashioned candle snuffer. If one were to place it down on top of these flames…

Just like that, they would go out, leaving behind only smoke.

"Can I help you?"

Laura jumped at the voice, spinning around to face the source of it, her heart pounding in her chest. Her hand even flew towards her gun, though she didn't draw it. She stopped herself when she saw him coming towards her out of the vestry, his black clothing and white collar a clear indication of his occupation.

"Hi," she said, trying not to give away the fact that her heart was still beating rapidly against her ribcage, making a deliberate attempt to physically relax herself. "Are you the Pastor here?"

"Yes, I am," he said, smiling gently. He was younger than she had expected, perhaps in his forties. "My name is Pastor Williams. And you are?"

"Laura Frost," she said, not quite sure why she wasn't using her official title. She hadn't even made the decision to skip it until the words were coming out of her mouth. "I'm interested in the candles. They kind of drew me in from outside."

"Ah, our memorial candles." Pastor Williams stepped closer, approaching the candles himself. His dark hair was only just shot through with gray at the sides, lending an air of distinction to an otherwise weak jaw and large nose. "Yes, they're very popular with our congregation. Do you know how they work?"

"I don't," Laura lied, because she wanted to hear it from him. She was interested in him, this Pastor. Because who would be better acquainted with the idea of candles and what they could represent than someone who actually worked in the church?

"Well," Pastor Williams said, with the kind of fatherly tone that Laura had noticed most priests tended to adopt, no matter the age of the person they were talking to. He reached out to take a long match from a stand beside the candles and lit it. "They represent the dead, for many of us. Or, rather, our prayers for the dead. When you light a candle, you think about a loved one who is now sadly departed, and you think of their soul in heaven. You pray that they are at eternal rest. You may even pray that you will see them again someday, when your souls are in the same place." As he spoke, he touched the match to three candles, one at a time.

"You keep them lit after the person has gone?" Laura asked.

126

"Well, of course," Pastor Williams said. "We want God to hear those prayers. And it's very reassuring for us to see that others have loved ones they are thinking of, too. When we approach these candles, we can feel the weight of all those prayers, all that goodwill. See how the flames continue to burn bright and strong? They represent more than just prayer. They represent life, purity, and the strength and brightness of our eternal souls."

"That's a lot of meaning to pack into a single flame," Laura said.

Pastor Williams gave a deep chuckle. "You may think so," he said. "I believe it's a kind of purification, keeping them lit. As they burn, they can take our worries with them. For the good of the church and for my parishioners, I like to let them burn as long as they can. To purify us all."

Three candles, Laura thought. He'd lit just three. No more, no less. Could it be that he was thinking of three people who had been lost in the town recently?

Three young women whose lives had been taken by someone who believed in the power that candles held?

"Did you know Evelina Collins?" she asked softly, watching him with a pasted-on innocence on her face, wanting to see his true reaction, trying not to make him suspicious about why she was asking.

The Pastor sighed sadly, his gaze flickering over the candles. Almost as if one of them was specifically for her. "Yes, I'm afraid I did. She was a regular member here at our services. Poor soul."

"What about the others?" Laura asked. Another test. She wanted to see if he knew their names. It wouldn't mean he was guilty, but if he didn't know who the latest victim was, then he might be innocent.

"Young Ashley hadn't been to services for a while," he said, shaking his head mournfully. "We always hope that the lost lambs will come back to the flock, but when something like this happens, it takes away that chance. I hope she'll find peace, wherever she is."

"Me, too," Laura said, actually meaning it. He hadn't mentioned the latest one, yet. Maybe he didn't know...

"The worst of them is Cici Powers," the Pastor said, sighing again. "Not long ago, I remember her standing up here and reading a poem during her father's memorial service. The poor mother is a widow and now bereft of a child as well. It's enough to test the strongest of our faiths. But I do believe she is with God now – and her father. That has to be something we can take as small comfort."

Laura let a respectful silence lie between them for a moment, but she wasn't done. Far from it. The new facts they had just added to the table were spinning inside her mind. One: all three victims had attended this church at one time or another, which finally gave her a concrete link between both the women *and* the precise type of candle left with their bodies. Two: this Pastor was also connected to all three of them by virtue of his connection to the church. Three: he was clearly obsessed with the candles, seeing something deep in their meaning.

"Were you here, when it happened?" Laura asked softly.

The Pastor sent a look in her direction, though it was far from a panicked one. "Why do you ask?" he said mildly.

"You're here now," Laura said, shrugging. "It was around this time that each of them was found, wasn't it? Or a little later, perhaps."

"You may be right, there," the Pastor conceded. "Yes, I was here. I'm always here. Tending the candles, waiting for someone to come in. You'd be surprised how often we have a visitor this late at night. There's no telling when someone will need the calming presence of God to reassure them, or to help them through a difficult time in their lives."

"Always?" Laura asked. "Don't you ever go home, Pastor?"

"I am home," he said, giving her a beatific smile. "My apartment is attached to the rear of the church. It's a solitary existence, but I am never alone. My God is always here with me."

Laura translated that in her head. The Pastor had no alibi. No one would be able to confirm that he was here on his own at the time that the murder happened. She doubted that anyone was going to accept the word of God as a testimony in court.

It felt kind of weird, accusing a Pastor. But Laura wasn't naïve. She knew that all kinds of people could be evil – and the church didn't exactly have a great reputation all the time. She had to do it.

" Pastor Williams," she said. "My name is Special Agent Laura Frost with the FBI. I need you to come with me to answer some more questions."

"Am I going to need a lawyer?" he asked, with the same placid calm.

Laura didn't know why she was so surprised. He'd probably known she was an agent from the moment she walked through the doors; news traveled fast in a town like this, after all. "You are entitled to one," she said. "At the moment, you aren't under arrest, and I'd just like to talk in a more formal setting."

"Then lead the way," Pastor Williams said. "I'm more than happy to tell you whatever you need – but I can tell you now, I had nothing to do with these dreadful killings."

Laura held out an arm, indicating for him to come along with her out of the church and towards her car. "Even so," she said, and she couldn't tell whether she was hoping to be right or not.

Because if she was right, then it was yet another example of a figure who should have been trusted betraying that trust and abusing his authority. But if she was wrong…

The killer was still on the streets, and the evening was not getting any younger.

CHAPTER TWENTY TWO

Laura rubbed her forehead, flipping through the pages of the file she'd prepared while Pastor Williams was waiting in the interview room. His record was predictably blank. She had crime scene photographs from the three dead women, designed to shock and awe him into confessing – or at least confront him with what he had done. There was very little else she could take into the room with her.

When interviewing a suspect, Laura always liked to be armed. To have something to put in front of them, facts to read off. It was a good way to corner them, to make them give in or at least make an accidental mistake. But with this case, she had hardly anything to go on. She picked up a few blank sheets of paper to pad out the file, just to make it look as though she had more than she did.

"You wouldn't have thought it to look at him, would you?" one of the local police officers – Mandy, Laura reminded herself – was saying as she walked by, deep in conversation with one of the men. Not Detective Waters – another one. Laura struggled to place him, but she had no idea what his name was. "All of that going on under the surface. I didn't even know he was accused of anything before."

That caught Laura's ear. "Excuse me," she said, holding out a hand to stop the two from passing her. "You're talking about Pastor Williams?"

Mandy nodded. "Yes, we just can't believe it."

"What was he accused of before?" Laura asked. "There's nothing on his record at all."

"Oh, I think it was informal," Mandy said, glancing at her colleague for confirmation.

He nodded. "Nothing was ever brought to us, but I heard it was taken to the church. To his superiors. There were a few local women who said he was a bit... you know. Inappropriate."

"Inappropriate, how?" Laura asked. She needed specifics, not vagaries.

"I'm not sure exactly," the male police officer said, shifting from foot to foot. "I just heard it was all hushed up."

130

"Well, who did you hear it from?" Laura asked, growing increasingly impatient. Were these rumors anything more than rumors? She needed something more concrete if she was actually going to use it.

He cast around, looking for someone else. "I think it was Frank who heard it first. He must be out with your Agent Won. He said the guy is into some really kinky stuff, too – like having hot wax dripped on him."

"Agent Won?" Mandy frowned, her expression one of total surprise and perhaps a little disgust.

"No, Pastor Williams," the man said. "He likes it when they use the church candles, apparently."

"And no one thought to mention this while we were looking for a murderer who left candles burning on his young, female victims?" Laura said, unable to stop the snap in her voice.

"Well," he said, looking a little taken aback. "I mean, Frank did mention it in passing."

Laura sighed and shook her head. "Evidence? Names, witnesses? Anything I can actually use?"

"You'd have to ask Frank," he said, shifting again, actually taking a step back.

"Great," Laura muttered, brushing past the two of them on her way to the interview room. It was all just hearsay, by the sound of things. They couldn't use hearsay. It wasn't helpful. At least she could bring it up as a way to get Pastor Williams to talk, but she'd hoped for a lot more than that.

She needed something that would help her to pin all of this on him and get him to confess, so that she knew she had the right man and could rest easy. So she could go home. Deal with Nate. Get ready for Lacey. Be there for Chris and Amy. Anything but having to watch the clock and wonder if another girl was already dead.

She walked into the room and put the file down on the table, taking a seat in the simple metal chair which she had grown to know as extremely uncomfortable. The only comfort in the matter was knowing that it was just as uncomfortable for the suspect – who, in this case, had chosen not to invite a lawyer along after all, and was sitting calmly with his hands folded in front of him.

"Agent Frost," he said affably. "Are we to begin our conversation now?"

"We are," she said, resting her hands on top of the folder and looking at him. " Pastor Williams, I'd like to ask you again whether

131

anyone can confirm your whereabouts yesterday evening – or the evenings of the Saturday and Thursday just past."

"I'm afraid there's no one," Pastor Williams said regretfully. "I was at the church, on my own. I have only God as my witness."

Laura took a breath, holding herself back from making some crack about Him not being able to take the stand. "There have been some disturbing accusations against you here in Pacific Cove," she said, wanting to lead with the angle of what she had just heard.

Now, for once, Pastor Williams blinked. "There have?"

"Yes," Laura said. She opened the file to one of the blank pages, tilting it towards herself as though she was reading. She wished she didn't have to use this tactic, because she didn't believe in following mere rumors. Yes, there was sometimes truth in them – but most of the time, they just hurt people and damaged communities. Still, with so much at stake, she couldn't leave anything off the table. "Inappropriate conduct towards your female parishioners, for one thing."

Pastor Williams frowned, though it wasn't quite as severe an expression as it might have looked on someone else. Given the lack of wrinkles on his youthful skin, in comparison to the gray in his hair, Laura couldn't help but imagine this was a man who frowned on very few occasions. "I haven't ever been accused of anything of that sort," he said. "At least, not that was ever brought to my attention."

"That's not the only thing a background check picked up," Laura said. "This is more of a rumor, but I understand that you enjoy the use of candles."

"I told you about that in the church," Pastor Williams said, with a half-chuckle. "I do believe they help to purify the soul. There's something about sending a prayer up to God and lighting that flame that gives a soul rest."

"I mean a little more than that," Laura said. She looked him right in the eye. "These women tell it that you enjoy having hot wax dripped onto your flesh. Is that the case, Pastor?"

Now he looked downright horrified for a moment – and then it lapsed into amusement. "That's certainly an original rumor," he said. "Unfortunately, there's no basis in truth to it. In fact, when I do accidentally get hot wax on myself as I tend to the memorial candles, I usually end up swearing. A vice which I must then apologize most profusely for to my Lord and Savior."

"I see," Laura said, though she kept her tone neutral. Better to let him wonder whether she believed him or not than to make it too obvious. "How do you think these rumors came to be?"

Pastor Williams gave her a benign smile, as though he was about to impart some common wisdom to a young parishioner who didn't have enough life experience yet. "In a small town like this, rumors are currency," he said. "I'm sure there are things said about most of the people who live here. As a Pastor, I'm more of a target than most. But there's no harm in it. Idle gossip never amounts to much."

" Pastor," Laura said, shifting and sitting more upright. "I'd like for us to stop wasting time. Tell me what you did to these women, and let's get them some peace. They can't rest properly until their murders are solved. Let's do that for them."

"I would love to help you with that," Pastor Williams replied calmly. There was no inflection in his voice, no hint that he had any worry or fear. "But I'm afraid I can't. I don't know who was responsible for these reprehensible crimes. I can only tell you that I was not involved."

Laura looked at him then, measuring. He was unflappable. There were only ever two reasons why someone was unflappable.

Because they were a sociopath and absolutely convinced there was no chance that they were going to get caught, or because they were innocent and knew they would be proved as such in due course.

Whichever option it was, Laura could tell already that there was no way she was going to get anything more out of him unless she had something real to bring to the table. The lack of alibi, the connection to the women, the connection to candles – it all fit. And yet, it was circumstantial. Not enough to even really consider arresting him over. A good lawyer, if he'd bothered to call one, would have him out of here within the hour.

"I'm going to discuss this with my colleagues a little further," Laura said, getting up. "I want you to really consider the implications of a confession. I know you're aware of how they can unburden the soul – and in this case, it could also get you a much reduced sentence. Do consider that, and if you decide you're ready while I'm out, all you have to do is let the officer posted at the door know."

She left him with those words in his head, just in case she was wrong, and he really was the killer. And she left, returning to the rest of the local police department in their one small room.

"I need everyone to stay alert," she announced to the room as a whole. "Until or unless we get a confession from Pastor Williams, we need to assume the killer is still at large. No one lets their guard down. Got that?"

CHAPTER TWENTY THREE

He sat in the shadows, watching the pattern that the candles cast on the floor.

It was a shame that the Pastor had been taken away. It really was. He'd watched it all from back here, where no one ever seemed to notice him. Not even the Pastor himself. He had a kind of talent for blending in with the shadows, not being seen. People would walk by him sometimes like he wasn't even there, even when he wasn't hiding on purpose.

The Pastor had always been very nice to him. That was one of the reasons he kept coming back here – for the Pastor's kind words. He liked to stand at the candles until the Pastor came out and then pretend that he'd only just arrived, just to hear something nice. And sometimes he would hide and listen to the Pastor saying nice things to other people.

You could learn a lot about other people that way.

But, still, he knew it was necessary. The Pastor hadn't done anything wrong, and someone would figure that out sooner or later. The church was safe in the meantime, because he was here, and he was sure that the Pastor would be able to handle it. And while the police were talking to the Pastor, it meant they weren't looking for him.

Not that they had done a very good job of looking so far – but he preferred it when they weren't looking at all. It meant that he only had to hide from the people that he didn't want to see him. Not from the police as well.

He looked up as she entered at last, just like she did every night. Cherry. She was always here on her way home from work. That was why he'd left the center of town and come out here early, so she wouldn't see him go in ahead of her. He'd been waiting a while – he guessed she got off late tonight, but it was a good job anyway, because he wouldn't have been able to do anything while the cop lady was here. He would have had to wait and let Cherry come and leave without him, and that would have been a terrible shame. They only had so long to connect on a deeper level, before the police got too suspicious, and he had to hide away from everyone.

It wouldn't matter too much, now that he had his new friends to keep him company. His loves. It was so nice to have people around him all the time now, people who were connected to him so deeply it could never be broken. And Cherry was going to be one of them. He'd known she had to be one of them for such a long time. It had come naturally to choose her as the next, before the risk of losing her became too great.

She went up to the candles like she always did, moving slow. She looked tired. He felt bad for her. It was alright. She was going to get enough rest, soon enough. She was going to rest forever, and all of this grief and sadness would go away. She wouldn't have to keep coming here to light candles for the one she had lost.

At least he knew she would understand. She did the candles too, so she must have known what they meant. What they did. How they could work for her and the one she had lost. How they would work for him, now. He liked to think that she would get it, if he told her what he was going to do.

Only, he wasn't going to tell her.

He reached into his pocket and silently drew out the rag he had stashed there. Behind it was the bottle, and he pulled that out as well, working fast but quiet. He was good at this. Had practiced it enough times. He set the bottle to the rag just as she was picking out a match to light her candle with, and he quickly stashed it away again as he stood.

He had to move fast, now. People didn't often notice him, but this was the most dangerous part of it all. If she turned around and saw him, she might scream, or else run away, and he wouldn't be able to catch up with her and she'd know. Everyone would know. That was why he couldn't make any mistakes.

He stole forward on light and silent feet until he was close enough. She'd lit her candle now, and she was staring into it, lost in memories. She had no idea that he was behind her.

Not until he was close enough to reach his hand in front of her and clamp the rag over her mouth, and by then, it was too late for her to do anything but struggle weakly for a single moment and then fall limp.

CHAPTER TWENTY FOUR

Laura sat at her desk in the precinct, holding her head in her hands, trying hard to think.

She'd had to yell at the last remaining cops who were still in the precinct until they were all on duty. Even their Chief had seemed reluctant to make them follow the orders. They were all casual and careless now, thinking they already had the right man in custody. The rumor mill together with the obviousness of a priest being obsessed with candles had done it for the Pastor's reputation, until it seemed like everyone just assumed they were going to get a confession sooner rather than later and put this whole business to bed.

All of which, frankly, terrified her. Not only were they complacent, but they were going to be looking for signs to reinforce their impression of his guilt as well. That could mean people ignoring evidence to the contrary. And with slip-ups like this Officer Frank never actually telling anyone from the FBI about the rumors he'd heard already happening, Laura felt like she was no longer able to trust anyone but herself in this investigation.

She didn't even know where Agent Won was.

Not that she particularly wanted to know. She was sure he was only chasing down his own harebrained theories, getting himself into trouble, and doing things she would be forced to reprimand him for. That was a headache she could do without.

But the headache she did have was one that she couldn't figure out how to get rid of. How to track down this killer. How to make sure that they did have the right man, even though she wasn't at all convinced they did.

She put her hands into the pocket of her jacket, slumping into her chair, and almost immediately a headache stabbed her in the temple. What was that for? Was that a normal, stress-related headache? Or was it a vision? She hadn't touched any-

Laura was staring into the flames. And she knew, now, exactly what she was looking at. The row of candles set up in the memorial stand in the church, several of them blazing, just as it had looked when she had left the church. Well, maybe not exactly. She hadn't memorized which ones were burning and which weren't.

But she knew where she was now. She was at the church.

As she watched, all of the flames went out suddenly, like they had been snuffed, plunging her vision into darkness and leaving no flames remaining. Only gray smoke trailed upwards, the only thing she could make out besides the pale white trunks of the candles, still standing in place.

She had seen the candle snuffer at the church, a metal tool designed for the purpose. But that wasn't this. This was something else.

This was all of the flames gone at once, with nothing moving between her and the flames.

What had snuffed them out? A sudden breeze? A gust? Someone blowing them out on purpose?

Laura came back to herself and the computer screen in front of her, a screensaver bobbing around on the monitor irritatingly. It reminded her that she was getting nowhere.

Except, maybe she was now. She'd seen the church. She knew where the candles were. None of which made much sense, unless the vision was trying to tell her that she *did* have the right person, and the church had been the place to look all along.

But then why would she still be seeing the candles, if they had nothing to do with the killer?

And what had triggered the vision, anyway? Laura knew that she wouldn't normally get any vision at all unless she was somehow in contact with something that would connect her to either the killer or the victim in some way. A hand on the gun that she was going to have to point at the suspect. A finger trailed along the wall of a house where the girl had been hidden away out of sight. A touch of the coffee machine that made the coffee that the stranger was going to spill when he walked back to his desk.

So, what was it this time, while she was sitting here with her hands in her pockets, touching nothing?

Maybe not nothing. Laura dug her fingers deeper into her pockets and found the crinkling cold plastic of an evidence bag, placed there earlier and forgotten about. She dug it out and found the strange burnt twig she had picked up at the last crime scene, next to Cici Powers's body.

She looked at it now in the light of the precinct, instead of a dark parking lot, and realized what she was actually looking at.

138

A match.

It was a match.

How could she have missed this before?

Laura studied it closely, bringing the plastic right to her face. It was so stubby and small, and burnt down completely, that she doubted it would have any evidential value in terms of fingerprints or DNA. The spot where the killer had held it, while using it to light the candle, had been passed over by the flame after he'd dropped it.

But that didn't mean it couldn't be useful. It was a small, thin match, the kind you bought in an individual matchbox or grabbed from a bar – cheap and nasty, and not very official. The matches she had seen Pastor Williams using at the church were a completely different make: long and thick, specifically designed for an environment where you might want to light multiple candles one after another.

Of course, that didn't mean Pastor Williams was exonerated by the match. It was, after all, more than possible for a person to use two types of matches. There was hardly a law against that.

But the vision had come back. Like someone was going to be blowing out those candles still. And the Pastor was in custody now. Of course, since these days her visions seemed to be breaking all the rules, it was possible she just didn't understand what she was seeing – but that didn't seem right.

None of it felt right.

Laura was used to following her gut. She believed in her gut. And she felt like she'd got the place right. The vision had shown her the church – she knew that now.

But what if it had led her to the wrong person?

There was only one way to be sure. She grabbed her cell phone and dialed Agent Won's number, listening to it ring out with an exasperated sigh. It hit voicemail, and she grabbed the keys to the rental car as well as her jacket as she walked out while leaving a message. "Agent Won, it's Agent Frost. I've brought in the Pastor from the church, though I think he's innocent. But he's given me a pretty good idea. I think the person we're looking for is connected to the church – in some other way. I'm going back there now. It's the one up by the cliff. I don't know what you're doing, but if you get this, come and join me. If we still haven't got the killer, that means he could be out there right now – and it's up to us to stop him."

She ended the message, striding out into the parking lot and back to the car, feeling at last like she might be on the right path.

She just hoped she wasn't far, far too late.

***

It was eerie, going back into the church on her own. Laura couldn't explain it, exactly, but there was something odd about it. Maybe it was the fact that she knew it was empty – or at least, that it was supposed to be empty. Having left the Pastor back at the precinct, it was like walking into his house without permission.

No, she realized; he lived here. This was exactly like walking into his house without permission, because she was. And maybe that shouldn't have concerned her as much as it did, given that she was an FBI agent. But normally she entered someone's home unannounced only for one reason: because she thought they were in danger, or were a danger themselves, and she had to take action.

But the church was very different. Laura walked in without her gun drawn, though she kept a hand close to her hip, ready. It was cold inside; the door swung open easily at her touch, and she realized that they hadn't quite fully shut it when she'd taken Pastor Williams away earlier. The old building seemed drafty at the best of times, but now in the middle of winter and with the door left ajar, it was freezing inside.

Still, the candles had withstood whatever breeze had come through. They flickered a few times as Laura approached them once more, her footsteps seeming strangely loud on the wooden floorboards. They were all still lit, still burning strong, just as they had left them.

No... weren't there more of them lit, now? Laura could swear it. Before, it had only been a few scattered flames, plus the three that Pastor Williams had lit. Now it was almost as though the whole rack was blazing, though there were still some gaps.

Pastor Williams hadn't been there.

Who had lit the candles?

Laura's heartrate skyrocketed with the realization that the open door meant anyone could have come in. And anyone might expect to be able to come in – after all, it was a church. The P Pastor's absence might not even have been noticed by anyone who came in to simply pray in peace. With three deaths in the town so recently, it was reasonable to think that people might be coming by the church more often.

Which did very little to reassure her, given that the killer themselves had to be somewhere in the town. And what better way to enjoy the spoils of their actions, all those lovely tears shed by the locals, than from a front row seat?

Laura bit her lip, swinging around and then completing a circle. She scanned every pew, every shadow, her eyes darting past the religious iconography and the furniture and trying to see any sign of someone else's presence. If the killer had been here – if they were here, now...

She saw nothing. But still, her heart was racing. The vision had shown her the candles being blown out. If it was the killer who did that, then she had to be in the place where he would be. She had no precise way to tell when the vision would come to pass, of course, but it had to be soon. Soon enough that it would be triggered at all.

If he came back, she would be right here, out in the open, with no backup.

It wouldn't have been the first time Laura put herself in harm's way for a case – far from it. She took her job seriously, and she took the duty of saving lives seriously. But she was also breaking FBI protocol pretty strenuously by going in without backup, and there was Lacey to think about. And Amy. And Nate, whose death she still needed to prevent. She couldn't do that if she was dead, herself.

Laura took a deep breath on purpose, steadying herself. She wasn't in mortal danger – not yet, anyway. There was no one here. But there had been, and she needed to find them before they found her. That was the best way to keep herself safe. With any luck, Agent Won would listen to his voicemail at some time this century and he would at least know where to find her.

Or her body.

Laura shook her head as if to forcibly rid herself of the thought, the eerie apprehension that seemed to have settled onto her bones since the moment she stepped foot inside the church. It was all around her, like she was walking through a haunted house attraction at Halloween, just knowing that someone was going to jump out at her and make her scream.

She put her hand on top of her gun just to reassure herself and began to look around some more.

The Pastor had told her that he lived here, in a small apartment at the back of the church. That was how he had put it. Laura looked up behind the altar, to where a small door led into the vestry. That was where he had come from, when she was here before. Maybe she could find something there. Evidence, perhaps. Because, she reminded herself, vision or no vision – Pastor Williams was still the best suspect she had managed to find so far.

She walked towards the door on cautious feet, creeping along, doing her best to tread lightly. A couple of the floorboards creaked as she stepped on them, each time making her pause and slow, listening hard for any sign of movement anywhere else in the building. The vestry door was ajar, but she couldn't see through it; she had no way of knowing what was on the other side.

Laura stepped up beside it and took a breath.

And then she pushed forward, swinging the door open and looking inside, her hand ready to draw that gun if she was going to need it.

The vestry, thankfully, was empty. Only a few items of clothing hung on a peg just inside the door – ceremonial items, by the looks of them. There was a bench which was presumably for the Pastor's comfort if he needed to dress, and a small desk which contained a Bible as well as a bundle of paper containing a typed-out sermon. Laura glanced over it quickly just in case, but it appeared to be something that the Pastor was working on in preparation for Christmas – nothing to do with candles, or death, or young women.

Laura stood in the center of the room and turned slowly, wondering if she had missed anything. But there was nothing. Just the door she'd come in from and another door that led in the opposite direction, and that one had to be the entrance to the apartment the Pastor had mentioned.

Laura drew her gun, because this time she wasn't going through that door unarmed. If someone was still in the building, and it wasn't the Pastor…

She didn't want to think about all of the possibilities of what she was about to find.

She braced herself against the wall beside the door, listening again. Nothing. But that didn't mean the apartment was abandoned. She reached out for the door handle, resting her fingers just on it for a moment as she worked herself up to it.

And then she turned it.

The resistance was immediately obvious. Laura pushed again, wondering if she was just at the wrong angle, but the door strained at one particular point not far from her hand. The lock. It was locked.

If the Pastor had locked it before she led him out of the church and drove him back to the precinct, then presumably no one could have got in since then. It was a dead end. At least, for now. Maybe she was better off waiting, seeing if someone else came in. It was entirely possible, according to what she had seen in her vision, that the killer simply hadn't arrived yet.

But it was as she was turning back towards the door out of the vestry that she saw it. A trap door, the kind that led down into a basement underneath the church. It was uncovered, but she hadn't seen it on her way in because it was half-hidden beside the desk.

If there was a door, that meant there was something behind it. An entrance or an exit. And if there was something behind it, then someone could be down there.

She wasn't done exploring yet.

CHAPTER TWENTY FIVE

Laura steadied the gun in her hands as she considered the door, figuring out how she was going to do this. It would have been better to call for backup, probably. But who was she going to rely on? The locals, who had gone down considerably in her opinion ever since they'd seen her bring in the Pastor and seemed to simply give up? Agent Won, who wasn't even answering his phone?

If Nate had been here, Laura would have waited. She'd have called him and known he would be there within minutes, and that she could go on with him as her backup. But he wasn't. And she couldn't stand there all night, waiting for someone to arrive. Not when there was still potentially a life on the line.

When there was no one to rely on but yourself, what did you do? You relied on yourself to get the job done.

Laura grasped hold of the heavy metal ring that served as a handle for the basement door and pulled, finding it surprisingly light. The door swung up and open, only clunking slightly as it hit the wall behind it. There was no creak of the hinges. They must have been well-oiled.

Which meant that someone went down here regularly – or at least, had gone down here recently. And when they went down, they preferred not to be heard.

Or was that paranoia talking, overlaying the whole scene with something darker than was really there? Wasn't it actually normal enough for a church to be well-kept, for someone to perform routine maintenance on it? And even if someone did regularly go down into the basement... for all she knew, *this* was actually the entrance to the apartment, and the door at the back she had found locked was simply a door to the outside.

Or maybe a creepy basement was a creepy basement, and Laura was just trying to tell herself everything she could to try to steady her own nerves.

She inched forward, looking over the edge of the hole, remaining cautious. The gun was down at her side, but easy to raise quickly if she should see something that sparked her instinct. There was nothing but a

144

ladder leading down into the basement space, down to another wooden floor, and a faint glow from somewhere beyond it.

A faint glow that flickered slightly as she watched.

Candles.

That settled it. There was no way Laura could stay up here when she'd been given such an obvious clue. She thought about trying Agent Won again but decided against it. She was here now. If she risked speaking on the phone, anyone who was down there would hear her – and the cell phone itself would be a distraction, something to reduce her reaction times.

She had to go down on her own.

Laura took a breath, uttering a quick mental prayer – since she was in Rome, after all – that she wasn't about to walk towards her own death. For the sake of her daughter, at least. It wasn't completely reassuring, but it would have to do.

She climbed onto the ladder and then swung herself around so that she was facing outwards, climbing in an awkward one-handed grip with her legs twisted. It was either that, or put her back to the room, and there was no way in hell she was doing that. She kept her gun in her right hand, away from the ladder, so that at least she had something to defend herself with.

Even so, it was a hair-raising moment. As she climbed down rung by rung, moving carefully and slowly, she was all too aware that anyone down there would have her in their line of sight before she saw them. She would be a pair of legs, then a torso, and a head last – and she would be exposed.

She found herself breathing heavier, short and sharp gasps, as she took each rung. With each step lower, she prayed she wasn't walking into danger. That she wasn't about to be shot, or stabbed, or have herself wrenched bodily from the ladder and thrown to the ground. At last, she descended far enough that she could duck her head and look.

It wasn't much of an improvement on being able to see nothing at all. The basement was a dark mess of furniture and perhaps adjoining antechambers, from what she could see in the vague flickering light. The candles were placed at random intervals: here on top of a spare, old desk, there on what looked like a broken pew, over there attached to an actual wall sconce. It was like descending into the past.

The walls were bare stone and brick, rough-looking and damp. It was colder down here than it had been up there, even with the night air flooding into the church. Laura shivered as she touched down on the

145

floor at last, straightening herself and casting around, trying to will her eyes to adjust to the dimness.

It was hard to focus. There was such a deep contrast between the light of the candles and the darkness between them, which seemed almost to be made of a thick substance with how deep the shadows became. And the light itself danced and flickered, making shadows move on every surface and in every corner, leaving Laura jumpy and tense.

She took in what she could see, which at this juncture wasn't much. There was a length of rope coiled up on a nearby table, though that meant very little. She hadn't seen any evidence of rope marks on the three victims so far, and the coroner's reports had not suggested they were in existence either.

Still, it didn't make her feel any better about being down here on her own.

There was also a low shelf which appeared to be stacked with cleaning supplies – all of them much more modern than the rest of the things she could see, which on closer inspection were threaded with dust and spiderwebs, clearly long-abandoned. There was bleach, several different kinds of spray bottles which held different cleaning fluids, a stack of sponges and clothes inside plastic packages, several packs of rubber gloves…

Why keep the cleaning supplies down here, if they weren't going to be used here? And they clearly hadn't been, because the place was filthy. There was only a kind of swath across the floor, an area where it looked as though feet must have passed time and time again, keeping the dust at bay.

Laura followed it with her gun held in front of her, on high alert for any sign of movement or sound.

It led between the desk and the table, through a kind of doorway into another part of the space. It seemed as though the whole thing had been subdivided at some point, perhaps into separate rooms to be used by the previous custodians of the church. It made for a confusing mess of a space, with openings seeming to come in every direction and no real way for Laura to know how much more of the basement there was to explore. She emerged into a new space which was altogether different from the first – a space that sent her heartrate skyrocketing once again.

It was set out with plastic sheeting. Plastic along the walls. Plastic across the floor. Plastic over every piece of old furniture, except for one, right at the far edge of the room. Another old desk, this one looking like something that might have been used in an old-fashioned school, perhaps as much as a century ago.

Laura was beginning to get the impression this basement was only used as a storage space – except for whatever it was that was being done here, now. It could have been that someone was trying to refurbish it and hadn't got very far yet.

So why did she feel a creeping sense of dread that that wasn't the case?

The interior of this room was also lit only by a few scattered candles, leaving everything cast in uncertainty and darkness around the edges. Laura stepped carefully, cringing as her feet hit the plastic sheet and made a clear crinkling noise. She hoped to God that no one else was down here – an ironic thought, she realized, given where she was.

She moved across to the desk on which she saw something shining dully in the light, pushed against the back wall. There were a number of tools lined up on it. A hammer, which was what had caught her eye. A mallet, a chisel that was so old and rusted it didn't shine at all, the broken handle of a saw. Construction tools, probably.

She hoped.

There was a strange space between the hammer and the mallet, as if something else was accustomed to lying there and had been removed. Laura lingered on that space for a moment, wondering.

There was no point in dwelling. She took one more glance around the strangely sterile room with all its plastic and hesitated. There were two more openings leaving this space: one right ahead of her beside the desk, and one to the left. She had no clues as to what lay beyond the shifting plastic sheets on either of them. She took a gamble, stepping forward through the nearest opening and brushing the sheeting aside.

As it turned out, Laura didn't need a vision to find the killer's next victim.

She was lying right there, on the floor of the next room.

Laura stumbled forward as soon as she saw the body of the woman, tied up and slumped on the floor on her back, her eyes closed. Her throat wasn't cut, but she was dead still – not moving at all – Laura dropped to her knees beside her, desperately fumbling towards her throat to feel for a pulse.

She concentrated hard, holding her own breath, trying to feel…

There!

Laura had made it in time – she was still breathing. Just unconscious. She quickly slipped a hand around the back of the blonde woman's head to feel for any damage, but there seemed to be done. If he was staying true to his MO, she was probably drugged.

There was no candle on her chest, no sign of any attempt to harm her beyond the ropes. Laura figured the killer must have knocked her out at some point before and brought her here, then tied her up in case she awoke while he was gone. That meant she had time, maybe.

She had a chance to save her life.

Laura grabbed her cell phone out of her pocket, having to put the gun down on the floor to do so. She stood, hearing the plastic which also covered the floor of this room crinkle underfoot even more as she did so. Her heart was hammering in her own ears so wildly. She scrolled through the list to Detective Waters's number, knowing that he would at least answer. She hoped he would answer. It was either that or she would need to go through 911.

The woman was so young, Laura couldn't help but think as she found the Detective's number in her contact list. So young. Maybe only her early twenties, just like the others. She didn't deserve to die right now, while she still had her whole life ahead of her.

Laura found the number, taking a couple of crunching steps back to give the girl space as she did so, and –

All she was aware of for a moment was the sensation of falling. In that space of time, which could only have been a split second but felt like so much more, she realized two things. The first was that she was about to hit the floor, though she did not apparently have enough time for her synapses to fire to instruct her body to save herself.

The second was that something had hit her hard over the head.

There was no third thing, because by the time Laura had made these two realizations, she was already losing herself to darkness – her consciousness spiraling away from her at the same rate with which the floor came up to meet her.

CHAPTER TWENTY SIX

Laura woke in pieces, little bit by little bit. The first thing was her head and the ache in it, which momentarily made her not want to wake up at all. Then there was light, dimly filtering through her eyelids and turning everything a dull red, until she realized that she could, in fact, open her eyes.

Awareness was among the last things to come back to her, but when it did, she immediately tried to move – and found that she could not.

This was a puzzle to work out. First, she tried again and had the same result, so Laura realized that something was holding her back. Something around her wrists, her legs, her back. She worked out that the thing holding her body was a chair, and then from the rough grazing feeling, she looked down to understand that she was tied with ropes.

One puzzle solved left another barrage of questions rising in her head. Where? Why? Who?

She slowly took in her surroundings; the light was dim but still painful to her eyes, seeming to increase the throbbing in the back of her head every time she so much as glanced in a new direction. Moving her head was another trigger. But she could move her head, which was good; she looked at the walls and realized she was in a room that she recognized, a room with strange plastic sheeting on the walls, a kind of ghostly room…

The basement.

She remembered it now: the basement under the church! She had been in here, looking at something – looking at her cell phone, because –

Because of the girl.

She looked down to the left and saw her, still laying exactly where she had been when Laura found her. She was still unconscious, or so Laura hoped. There was no sign that anything new had been done to her.

How long had it been? Down here, it was impossible to know. There was no way to see the outside, and even if she could have, Laura remembered it had been night already when she ventured down. If it was still night, she wouldn't be able to know whether it had been five minutes or five hours.

For the sake of her own skull, she hoped it had been five minutes. Or even less. She knew how dangerous it could be to have a head injury that knocked you out for longer than that, and with the way her head was throbbing...

A noise behind her made Laura flinch, letting out a startled cry. That was when she realized she was not gagged, which was a relief in itself – but an extremely short-lived one. Because the sound from behind her came again, and she recognized it as the sound of a footstep crunching across the gathered plastic.

Someone was behind her.

She froze, her eyes going as wide as they could as if more light could somehow help her see through the back of her own head, trying to stay still and keep her breathing under control. If he didn't realize she was awake...

She needn't have bothered. A man stepped around in front of her, dressed in shabby blue overalls and with his hands stuffed in his pockets. He looked her right in the face and showed no surprise at all that she was looking back. He must have known she was awake already.

Laura fought against the ropes that held her arms down, struggling, trying to get free. All he did was look at her, his head cocked at an angle like he was curious. He was such a nondescript man, the absolute worst nightmare for a cop who needed to describe a suspect: brown hair receding from his hairline, a weak chin, thin lips, a nothing of a nose. Nothing about him was strong or memorable. Even his eyes were a little watery. Laura figured he was in his late thirties, but with that hairline he could have been older; with those eyes he could have been younger. It was almost impossible to say.

Laura stopped struggling and just looked back at him. The ropes weren't coming loose. Now that she'd had more than a moment to live with the situation, to understand how much danger she was in, she tried to calm down. Panic wasn't going to get her anywhere, here.

But she was a damn good FBI agent, and she had a lot of tools in her arsenal when it came to negotiation and investigation. Maybe, if she stayed calm, she could talk him into letting her go – or at least, letting his guard down.

"Who are you?" she asked, softly, moderating her voice on purpose. Making it a curiosity, not an accusation.

150

"I work here," he said, by which Laura gathered he must have meant the church. "You've seen me, you know."

"I have?" Laura said, blinking. She tried to place him. Maybe if he was wearing different clothes...?

"Up there," he said, raising his eyes towards the ceiling momentarily. It was a curious gesture, especially in a place like this. Like he was talking about heaven, not just the church. "And elsewhere. I live here in town. You've walked past me a dozen times."

"At the places where the women were found?" Laura asked. She had enough of her wits about her still to avoid the words 'crime scene.' Anything that might trigger him. Killers didn't tend to enjoy hearing about the fact that they were killers. It might make him angry. Especially if he saw what he was doing as art, or ritual, or a necessary act.

"And others," he said, straightening his head. He began to move around the space, with a slow, careful walk that barely produced any sound from the plastic sheeting. Laura realized that he must have been making sound on purpose a moment ago, or she wouldn't have heard him so clearly. No wonder he'd been able to sneak up behind her, given how much noise of her own she had been making at that point.

Laura took advantage of him turning his back on her, ambling around to some other part of the room that was mostly hidden in shadow, to look down at herself and try to assess what she had. Her ankles were tied to the legs of the chair, and her wrists were bound to the arms. But it wasn't a plastic chair, or a new one. It was wooden. That was something. Maybe something she could use. And she wasn't sure she was looking at the kind of knot a professional would tie, either – there were just two loops of the rope around each hand, with the knot orientated on top of her wrist. No loop around her chest or between her arms to hold her more securely.

"You know," he said, making her snap her head up and pay attention again. "It's funny. People just don't see me."

"They don't?" Laura asked, trying to keep him talking. If he wanted to chat, she was happy to. It meant she wasn't dying. "I can see you now."

"Yes, but I've brought attention to myself this time," he said, with a kind of self-effacing smile in her direction. "You didn't notice me before. Not even Pastor Williams notices me most of the time, and he's the one who hired me to take care of the maintenance."

151

"That's the work you do?" Laura asked. "That's why you have access to this basement?"

"No one else ever comes down here," he said, then made an 'ah' sound and reached for something that was hidden on a shadowy shelf by the door, far from the nearest candle. It seemed he'd been looking for something. Whatever it was, it disappeared into his pocket quickly. "Not even the Pastor. I can't say I like it too much myself, but I make do. With the police patrolling more up there, I have to spend as much time down here as I can."

"Why don't you like it?" Laura asked. It was probably an inane question, but the more she understood about him, the better.

He only looked at her with a kind of pitying expression on his face, as if he could see right through what she was attempting to do. He glanced around then at the plastic-clad walls, the decaying old furniture, and the cobwebs, as if to convey that there was plenty not to like about the place.

He moved out of sight for a moment into the other room, and Laura took advantage of the moment to start wriggling her hands. Not pulling up against the ropes or trying to force them but slipping her limb into the right place to slide right out of them. They were still too tight, even when she took it slow. She quickly relaxed her arms, pretending that she hadn't been moving at all, as he stepped back through the plastic-curtained doorway.

"You know, my mother died recently," he said. It was like they were just chatting away while standing and looking out over the sea at an observation point, two strangers who might as well shoot the breeze together. There was no hurry about his movements, no panic in his voice. Everything was so matter of fact.

"I'm sorry to hear that," Laura said, almost automatically.

"Yes, well," he said, as if that was to be expected but also not entirely needed. "Funny thing was, we were never very close, my mother and I. Even though we lived together for so long. I suppose we just didn't connect in that special way in life, whatever the reason was."

Laura's ears had pricked up. She swallowed uneasily. "In life?" she asked, unable to stop herself.

"No, well, it wasn't her fault," he said, casting about for something on a table at the other side of the room. Laura heard a clink and saw a familiar shape and saw that he was arranging the tools she'd seen before. He must have carried them through. "Nor mine, I don't really think. But sometimes it happens that way. Anyway, it was after she died that it all started with the candles."

"Did you light one for her?" Laura guessed. It wasn't a hard leap to make, but she hoped she was right. If she was going to have any chance of getting out of this, they needed some kind of rapport. Something to make him relax, or even change his mind. She wasn't just going to go down like this. She needed to get him on her side.

"As soon as she was taken away, I came down here and lit a candle," he said. He picked up a candle now, an unlit one, and moved purposefully across to the other side of the space. "She lit one for my father, you see. So, I thought she'd like it. And after I lit it, I didn't want it to go out. I kept it at home, and I kept it burning. And every time it was almost about to go out, I'd take another and light it from the same flame and keep it going."

He did the very action he was describing now, lighting the candle from one which was set into the wall. He carried it over then, closer to Laura, and she couldn't help but flinch. She didn't want that candle anywhere near her. Not if he was going to do what she thought he was going to do with it.

Instead, he set it down on a ledge she hadn't noticed, covered as it was with the plastic. Smoothing it out carefully so that that candle wouldn't fall, he took his time, turning slowly afterwards to face both Laura and the unconscious girl on the floor.

"Do you know, this is going to be very strange," he said. "I've never had an audience before."

"Then why have one now?" Laura asked. "You might as well let me go."

He only smiled, like he was trying to tell her he wasn't going to fall for that one. "Do you know what happened after I lit that candle?" he asked. "The one for my mother, I mean. It was so very odd. I started to feel something."

"What was it?" Laura asked. She was trying to keep him distracted, but it didn't seem to be working. He wiped his hands briefly on his overalls and then pulled out a pair of gloves, almost as an afterthought, and slipped them on. Workman's gloves, oversized and padded, that made his hands look bigger than they were. Laura's heart was beating so fast it was making her feel dizzy. Those gloves meant he was about to get to work, and time was running out.

"I was close to her at last," he said, pausing for a moment to give a little wistful sigh. "Really close to her, in a way we never were when

153

she was alive. I felt this genuine connection. She would come to me at night and talk to me and listen. Even just to feel her around all the time – it was so comforting. And she never would have been so gentle with me before it happened. After the candle went out at last, she stayed with me anyway. I knew, then, what I had to do. You see, I've never really been close to anyone. People don't notice me, and when they do, they don't have a lot of interest. I'm just like a piece of furniture, for the most part. I might be tolerable to have around, but people don't think about me, and they certainly don't want to talk to me."

"I'm sorry to hear that," Laura said carefully. "You know, you never told me your name."

"Robert," he said, and then bent and set his hands under the unconscious girl's armpits and began to drag her towards the center of the room.

Laura sat forward in her seat, as much as she was able to, alarmed. Where was he taking her? Was he about to kill her? Laura couldn't let that happen – it was the very thing she'd come here to stop. But on the other hand, if he took her into the other room, maybe this would be her chance to get free...

But Robert stopped when he reached the middle of the room they were in, letting the girl drop gently back into a position where she was lying on her back, almost peacefully. Except that her sleep was artificial and unwanted, and if she woke up here, Laura knew she would feel anything but peace.

"Robert," Laura repeated, using the power of his name, trying to get him to listen to her and talk to her instead of doing whatever it was he wanted to do now. "Is that what this is all about? Feeling close to people?"

"That's precisely it," he said, with a sad tone in his voice. He looked at the unconscious girl for a moment longer, as though satisfying himself that she was in the right place. "You may think very little of me. I accept that. But you know, for people like me, there are very few options. You get to a place where just a little human interaction is all you need. All you crave. Where you would do anything for a little affection. And all of these women – Evelina, Ashley, Cici, and Cherry – each of them were people I saw in my daily life. Women I admired so much. And do you know how often they noticed me?"

"I'm sure they noticed you more than you realized," Laura said. "We all interact with people in different ways. If you were a customer

154

at the diner, I'm sure that Ashley would have recognized you more than you thought. I'm sure she knew who you were."

"I've lived here my whole life," Robert said with a sigh that seemed to come from deep in his soul, moving back over to the table where he had placed the tools. There was a hunched stiffness to his movements, like he was cradling a great pain inside of him. "And no one ever remembers my order. Not even when I order the same thing day after day after day. You know, there are people who can arrive in a town fresh off the bus and within a week, people are offering to serve them 'the usual.' I don't know how they do it. It's like some kind of magic to me, and it comes so naturally to everyone else."

"I think people will notice you a lot more now," Laura said, which came out darker than she intended. It was true, though. He would gain himself notoriety with this. Probably not in a positive way. She could imagine him being paraded and celebrated as a champion of the incels. She didn't voice any of this, though – the last thing she needed was for him to realize that she wasn't really on his side.

"I don't need them to," Robert told her, in a voice that was soft, almost dreamy. "I already have everyone I need. We're so much closer now. Like this, I can carry on."

"You mean, you're done?" Laura asked. Hope sprang fitfully in her chest. It wasn't good news to be down here with him, obviously, and she wanted to save the girl he had in front of him – Cherry, he'd called her. He was moving back towards her now, holding something in his hands, his back to her. But even if she and Cherry died here – if he was done – if he wasn't going to kill again after this...

"I don't know about that," he said, making her heart drop again. "Maybe there will be others, in the future. Maybe I'll meet someone new. And, of course, I haven't finished with Cherry yet. Or you."

"Me?" Laura breathed, her voice catching in her throat. It wasn't as though she'd thought he would let her go. But still...

He turned, the dancing golden light of the candles reflecting off the thing he had in his hands. It was a knife. Long and wickedly sharp, with a polished shine to it that suggested it had been cleaned and whetted recently. "Well, of course," he said, mild as ever. "I have very much enjoyed talking with you. It's been so long since I could be open with someone like this. I thought I was unlucky when you walked in just as I was getting ready to set up things with Cherry, but it gave me some more time to admire her as she is, to remember her. And then I realized you could join me, too. And once it's all over, we'll be connected in a way that is so deep and strong. You'll see. We'll have all the time in the world to talk some more after that. And I'll find somewhere nice to leave you both, after. You can lay in rest together. Maybe on the beach, where you can hear the waves and look up at the stars."

"Robert," Laura said, gasping for breath. She felt like she was being held underwater. She couldn't see straight anymore. There was only one thought in her mind. *Lacey.* Her daughter. She thought of her daughter growing up without a mother. "You don't have to do this. We can talk as much as you like now. Why rush? We might as well talk some more while we can do it face to face."

"Don't worry," he said, with almost a chuckle in his voice. He squatted down beside Cherry, holding the knife by her neck, like he was measuring where he was about to cut. "It's quite alright, you know. It's only a moment, and then you'll be with me. You'll feel what I feel. Everything will be okay, and we won't need to communicate in the traditional ways anymore. It goes far beyond that."

"But what about talking to everyone else?" Laura blurted out, trying to find some way to distract him, but it was no use. He was bending over Cherry completely now, stroking her hair back from her face, moving it away from her neck. He had some kind of dish that he'd carried with him, a basin, and Laura realized with a sick terror that he was planning to use it to catch her blood as it drained from her neck.

She struggled against the ropes, but it was useless. There was just enough give for her to kind of shuffle up and down in place, making the chair move just slightly, but nothing else. She couldn't pull her hands back or out or break through the knots. They were almost cruel: loose enough to give her hope, but tight enough to make the hope a vain one. She couldn't get out. She couldn't fight it.

She was going to die here.

"Agent Frost?"

The calling of her name made them both freeze, Laura and Robert at the same time. In shock, they both stared in the direction the sound had come from. The same direction Laura had come from. The side of the basement where the stairs gave out.

CHAPTER TWENTY SEVEN

Laura had never closed the basement trap door behind her. Robert must not have done it, either. Whoever came into the church would have seen it, and probably decided it was the obvious place to climb down.

Especially given that the person who had come into the church was Agent Won – and he had been expecting to meet Laura there.

Laura opened her mouth to call back to him, but a flash of movement caught her eye – Robert, holding the blade right at Cherry's throat, fixing her with a sharp look. She understood his meaning well enough. It was a warning.

Shout, and Cherry dies.

Laura clamped her lips shut, her palms sweating as she turned them against the arms of the chair, trying to get some purchase on something. This was going to end badly, she knew. How could it not?

Agent Won didn't stay put near the stairs, simply waiting for her to reply. As much as she prayed he would, apparently you had to be inside the actual church to have your prayers heard and answered, because she heard his footsteps coming closer across the plastic sheeting in the room next door. He even muttered a quick, "What the hell?" half under his breath as he took in the sight; there was a moment of pause in his movements, then a couple of quick crunches, and Laura could picture him spinning in a circle, looking around at everything.

No, she realized: she didn't need to picture it. Even though the light was shifting and deceptive, she could just about make him out on the other side of the plastic curtain. A dark shape, moving, pausing for a moment longer, and then –

And then moving forward, towards the curtain that separated them.

Laura squeezed her eyes tight shut for a single moment and then opened them again, the physical violence of the movement sending a fresh wave of pain through her head that she barely felt. She was too focused on him. On trying, mentally, to send him some kind of message to go back. To stop. To call for help, or something.

Or to be smart, somehow, and stop all of this from happening. But not even Laura could see how he could make that work.

157

He was walking too fast for her to think, coming through the curtain too fast for her to know what to do – and then Robert was springing up from where he was crouched over Cherry, moving even faster towards Eric, putting them on a collision course –

There was a sickening crunch of plastic and metal and bone as they came together, and for a moment Laura couldn't even tell what had happened. Then there was a shot, echoing so loud in the tiny space that she couldn't hear a single thing afterwards, and a clatter, and by the time she'd blinked her eyes to realize what was going on they were both on the ground. Eric had blood streaming from his left shoulder, and his gun had fallen out of his right hand – not near him, but over near Laura, where it had dropped and then skittered along the wooden floor. The shot he'd fired had gone wide, no doubt embedding itself somewhere in the thick floorboards. Robert was uninjured, but they were fighting, and Eric was already at a disadvantage with his wound, and Laura was helpless to do anything but watch.

No... not helpless.

She could move the chair.

She shuffled it hard, pushing as much as she could with her feet, even lifting her body off the seat momentarily with the force required to move the chair more than a hair's amount at a time. She pushed and strained with everything she had, glancing behind herself and then at the two fighting men, behind herself and then at them...

She reached the spot she was aiming for and swung to the side, spinning the chair a good ninety degrees to get alongside it. The candle. One of many that were burning around the sides of the room. It was just at the right height, though that had hardly been intentional – it had burned down almost to a stub. If she could just position herself exactly right...

Eric grunted with pain as Robert got a shot into his face, the unmistakable crunch of a fist meeting a nose, and Laura redoubled her efforts. She couldn't stop herself from crying out as she overshot with one last heavy shuffle, the flame touching her skin. She jerked her hand back as much as she could, though with the restraint of the ropes it wasn't enough. The heat was almost unbearable. It took everything she had, everything, not to move. She thought of Lacey's face. She held the image for as long as she could before the burning of her skin took it away from her.

Laura focused on the sounds coming from the other side of the room, the dull thud of fists hitting flesh, trying to let that distract her from the pain. From the burn. Her head whipped round to look at them, not at the damage she was doing to herself. Eric got a punch into Robert's side, but Robert simply rolled and pulled away and, when Eric tried to follow, Robert used his momentum against him to throw his bleeding shoulder against the floor, making him cry out. She kept pulling her wrist, pulling it as far away from the candle as she could –

It gave way, her whole arm flying across her body with the momentum of her pressure, free at last. The candle had burned through the rope that was holding her.

There was a nasty blister already forming on the side of her hand, but she ignored it, sparing just one glance for Eric and Robert and then renewing her efforts to reach for the rope around her other wrist. Eric was on his back now, struggling, trying to fight one-handed while he clutched the injured arm against himself. There was blood everywhere, everywhere, impossible to tell what was his and what was Robert's, what came from his shoulder or what came from their faces or even their cut knuckles.

And Robert had him pinned down –

And Robert was reaching for the knife that he had dropped a moment before, which had fallen close by them.

No.

She couldn't let it happen.

Laura pulled the strand that would loosen the ropes on her other arm and yanked her wrist free with so much force it hurt, even as the ropes gave way, and she reached for her gun. The holster was empty. *Of course the holster was empty.* There wasn't time to figure out where her gun was now. Eric's was lying on the floor. She dove, going down on her knees, letting the chair clatter after her where it was still tied to her ankles, not caring, not paying attention to the pain as it fell on her legs, just grabbing the gun –

Lifting it –

Aiming –

Robert's hand on the knife, the flash as he raised it high, the last struggle as Eric fought to upset his balance and push him off –

The recoil from the gun ricocheted through her hand, and for a moment after the loud bang and the smell of smoke and the flash, Laura wasn't sure she'd done it. Robert was sitting there, like nothing had happened, the knife still in his hand. He swayed slightly. In the moment, all Laura knew was a dreadful fear that she'd missed, that the

159

knife would plunge down into Eric's chest or throat before she could aim and fire again.

And then, slowly, like she was watching some melodramatic movie, Robert toppled sideways to the floor, and Laura knew that he was dead.

CHAPTER TWENTY EIGHT

Laura looked up dully as Eric walked over, sitting down beside her on the tailgate of the ambulance. They were both sutured and bandaged and dosed, wrapped in foil blankets to keep off the chill of the middle of the night.

The air had that kind of unreal quality to it that always seemed to settle in during the early hours, if you were still awake. Everything still around you, except yourself. The way the night washed all of the colors out of everything. And here, it was even stranger, because there was so much activity happening right in front of them, and the colors that had been leeched out were replaced by blue and red, flashing over and over again.

Maybe it was just that the adrenaline had worn off. Or maybe it was the painkillers they had given her. Whatever it was, Laura couldn't help feeling like something about this just wasn't real.

"How's your hand?" Eric asked.

Laura looked down at her hand, stupidly, as if the bandages could tell her. "I'm not sure," she admitted, with a high, uncharacteristic laugh that made her feel even more on edge than she had before. When had she ever made a sound like that before? "I can't really feel it anymore."

"They got you on the good stuff, too, huh?" Eric said, snorting and shaking his head. She looked up at him and laughed, and for a moment they were both laughing, and something kind of cleared from her. Like a net being lifted up from over her eyes.

Their laughter died down to nothing, leaving the hush of the night only to be disturbed by the local cops and EMTs and the residents standing around on the street in their nightclothes. It felt like poison on Laura's lips, now the impulse was gone. The community around them was shattered. Three young women dead, and one no doubt traumatized for life – and Laura herself had ended a life. Even if it was a dangerous and violent one, it had been a life.

It was never going to be enough, no matter how many cases they solved. There would always be men like Robert out there. Men who would kill and kill again. The heaviness of it sat on her shoulders, a burden that would never be removed no matter how hard she worked.

Laura looked at Eric, and actually saw him for what was probably the first time. A young, eager, enthusiastic agent. A man who wanted to make a difference and had signed up to risk his life for it. Because that was how almost all of them were, at the start. Thinking they were going to save the world and all the people in it, and be a hero, and maybe have a biopic made about them one day. Until they got put into a situation like this and had to actually risk themselves, which was the point when most agents realized they could admit to themselves they were actually in it for the money and the glory.

But Special Agent Eric Won had made it through that moment, and he'd done so as a hero. Coming to her aid, walking right into danger, and then fighting off a serial killer to save her. She'd saved him, in turn, but that didn't negate what he had done. She owed him her life. If it wasn't for his distraction, she never would have been able to get free.

For that reason, at least, she figured she could drop her ridiculous grudge against him for the simple crime of not being Nathaniel Lavoie.

"Thank you," she said. "For coming when I asked you to. If you hadn't arrived, I'm sure it would have ended much more badly."

Eric nodded, but there was a humbleness in it. "I'm just sorry I didn't pick up the phone when you rang," he said. "I was off chasing down a wild goose, as it turned out."

Laura sighed, mentally telling herself she had to give him at least some praise. "At least you were chasing," she said. "I can see how much this job means to you. How seriously you take it."

"I've just been a bit… overzealous, haven't I?" he said, scratching the back of his neck with a sheepish expression. The sling holding his other arm in place, to stop him from aggravating his shoulder injury, shifted as he did so. He looked rather worse for wear, with a splint on his nose and bruising around one of his eyes, underscored by an angry-looking cut on his lip. "I'm sorry about that."

Laura chuckled lightly, shaking her head. There was a kind of odd feeling in the back of her skull, where Robert had hit her. Like pain should be there, but she just couldn't feel it thanks to whatever they had given her. The EMTs had checked her over and told her she was fine for now, but that she had to rest as much as possible and go in for a CT scan before flying home. She wasn't looking forward to the trip to the hospital. She just wanted to be at home, curled up in bed.

162

"You'll be alright," she said. "You'll learn the ropes and make a good agent of yourself. And now you've got an impressive war wound to show off if anyone ever questions your investigative style."

"I hope I'll learn some more of them from you," Eric said, with a look of affection that was wholly unexpected. It was like he was looking up to her – as a possible friend, maybe a mentor. But then, going through something like this could bond two people. Laura supposed she couldn't be surprised by it. "I'd like to be partnered up again sometime in the future. I get the feeling there's a lot more you could have taught me this time, too, if I'd been listening more."

Laura smiled, giving a modest wave of her hand. "At least you've figured that much out," she joked.

"I've just heard from the team at the hospital!" Detective Waters had bounded up beside Eric, making Laura turn and squint at him. She was so tired. And she probably should have gone for that scan and everything else earlier, but she'd wanted to stay and make sure everything was wrapped up here. "Cherry Mackintosh is awake and well. She's just recovering from the after-effects of the chloroform, and she should be back to normal completely. No lasting injuries."

"That's excellent news," Laura said, resting her heavy head against the inner wall of the ambulance. "Thank you, Detective Waters."

"Thank you," he said, fervently. "I don't know what we would have done if you guys hadn't come out here."

"Just doing our jobs," Laura told him, smiling faintly. She could really do with a rest.

"I think we should probably get to the hospital, now," Eric said, casting around for the EMT who had stayed with them to check over their wounds in person. "Don't you think so, Agent Frost?"

"Sure," Laura agreed breezily, letting the flow happen around her. She was sure it wouldn't hurt if she just closed her eyes for a few minutes.

***

Laura took another sip of her coffee, nodding into it. The chintzy music playing in the restaurant felt like it was wrapping around her, like a blanket, soothing away the awfulness of the story she'd just told.

"Seriously?" Chris said, shaking his head in wonder again. "I can't believe it. You were only gone for a few days. Your life is so..."

163

"Please don't say exciting," Laura grimaced. A week of bed rest after coming home from California had been the very opposite of exciting. She'd even had to skip her weekend with Lacey, much to her dismay. But at least it had given her the chance to think about a few priorities – and reorganizing this date with Chris had been one of them.

"I was going to say eventful," he replied, raising his eyebrows. "You could have died. I know first-hand how serious head injuries can be."

"I thought you were a cardiologist," Laura teased.

Chris rolled his eyes playfully. "I still had to do rounds when I was a resident," he said.

"Do you remember that far back?" Laura retorted, immediately wondering if she'd pushed it too far. But he only laughed incredulously, setting his own coffee cup back in the saucer and shaking his head at her.

"Are you calling me old, Ms. Frost?" he asked. "I don't know if you got that, but that's a doctor thing – I just called you 'Ms.' because you're too also old for me to assume you're a Miss."

"How cutting," Laura said, clutching her heart in mock pain with a grin that didn't quite match. She was glad he could give as good as he got. She'd already worked out that Chris was only a handful of years older than her but being able to joke around together was important. Especially if this first date was going to lead to a second.

And it showed her something else, too. That he wasn't his brother. She'd already known that, yes, but any lingering doubts she had were getting smaller and smaller the more time they spent together. He looked nothing like John, he spoke nothing like John, and he didn't act like him, either. John would probably have cracked a wine glass in his fingers at being disrespected like that. Even if he had restrained himself under public scrutiny, Laura was sure that there would have been a flash of rage in his eyes, a warning for later when they were alone.

But Chris just laughed and smiled along with her, and Laura felt that reassurance settling into her chest more and more with each moment.

"Here's your check, sir, madam." That was the waiter, who had reappeared beside their table with the kind of fleet-footed silence that you expected in a nice restaurant like this. A restaurant which Laura still felt was far, far too nice for someone like her to be sitting in – but Chris had insisted that it was his treat. She wasn't sure how to feel about the possibility of getting used to that.

164

Chris turned to the waiter with a smile. "Thank you." When the man was gone, Chris picked up his coffee cup again and studied it briefly. "Though it will be a shame to get out of here. I've had a good night."

"So have I," Laura admitted. She smiled as their eyes met, then found herself actually blushing a little. Like she was a schoolgirl or something. She hadn't met eyes with a man and blushed like that since back when she started dating Marcus.

Given how that marriage had worked out, she wasn't sure if that was a good sign or not.

"We should do it again," Chris said, with a kind of put-on casual air that was transparent, showing his nervousness underneath. "Next week, maybe, after the girls have their play date on the weekend."

"Sounds good to me," Laura said, finishing her coffee and setting it down. "That is, assuming there isn't another killer out there who wants to ruin my social life for the second time in a row."

Chris laughed, but then his expression fell. "Was that serious?"

"Only slightly," Laura said, shaking her head ruefully. "Unfortunately, it's a reality of the job. I do sometimes have to leave at the drop of a hat, and I can be gone for days or even weeks in some cases."

"Well," Chris sighed, tilting his head in a kind of shrug. "I guess, having a doctor's schedule, I can't really complain about that."

"No," Laura smiled. "You can't."

"I'll walk you to your car," Chris said, then paused. "Unless you think that's a bit too old-fashioned?"

"Not too old-fashioned at all," Laura said, even though it was a little bit – because she also thought it was a sweet gesture, and maybe it was about time she spent time with a man who wanted to treat her like a lady. She stood, picking up her purse while he waited for her to settle it on her shoulder. He stepped aside to let her lead the way, even though he was in front of her. She walked through the restaurant and outside with the feeling of him behind her all the way, like a physical presence even though he wasn't touching her. It sent an itch down her spine that she badly wanted him to scratch.

Out by the car, they paused and lingered, Laura crossing her high heels on the parking lot tarmac and feeling a little bit lost, a teenager again. Chris put his hands in his pockets and looked up at the sky as if to say what a lovely clear night it was, and sighed, and then they looked at each other and burst out laughing.

165

"I don't know why I'm being so awkward," he confessed. "You'll have a good few days until I see you again, won't you? And drive safe. Especially with that head injury of yours."

"You know I'm all better now," Laura said, pleased to hear that he cared all the same. She only winced when she took out her car keys, grazing the side of her still-bandaged hand on the inside of her coat pocket.

"All the same," Chris said, then hesitated, and then seemed to come to a decision. He stepped forward, one hand resting on the side of her shoulder, and kissed her on the cheek. "Be careful."

"I will," Laura breathed, and he hadn't stepped back yet, so when their eyes met, they did so across a much shorter space than usual. And when they did meet, it was clear, very clear to both of them that a kiss on the cheek was not going to be enough.

Laura tilted her head up and looked at his mouth, and he didn't need hinting twice. Chris closed the distance between them a second time, their lips meeting and sending a thrill of heat through her despite the winter cold.

When he pulled back and stepped away again, they smiled and chuckled at each other, and he made a gesture back towards where he'd parked his own car. "Well, I'll…"

"Sunday," Laura said, rescuing him with a word they could both agree on.

"Sunday," he agreed, grinning at her one last time before moving away.

Laura got into the car and sat for a moment, smiling stupidly out at the windscreen – or rather, not really at anything at all. She giggled to herself, then covered her mouth in a kind of pleased shock at the sound she'd made.

Was this really her? A year ago, she'd been so broken. She'd been divorced, unable to see her own daughter, and only really friendly with the inside of a bottle. She'd dragged herself home every night only to lose herself in oblivion so she could forget, and then in the day she'd had to drag herself hungover to work and try to make a difference even though she felt like she was the most useless woman in the entire world. And the visions would come, and then she'd want a drink again before midday, and Nate had to put up with her being snappy and slow until she did.

It had almost put an end to their partnership back then, she remembered. Before she'd managed to start pulling herself up out of the gutter, one lost sobriety chip at a time. He'd stuck by her, though.

But apparently, this time was different.

Laura reached inside her purse to dig out her cell phone, more out of habit that anything else. She knew by now that she wasn't going to see a message or a missed call from Nate. If he was going to call, it would have been when she was recovering from her head injury. But he hadn't even messaged to wish her well. That was how she knew just how completely serious he still was about never working together again.

Never being friends again.

The thought put a bit of a dampener on the elation that kiss had produced.

She scrolled through the messages on her phone to the last one she'd sent him, before she'd even gone on the last case. It was still unanswered, even though it was marked as read.

And a spike of pain in her head for a moment had her panicking, thinking that she must have triggered her concussion again – but then she realized it was in her temple, not in the back of her skull – the same place that her visions always –

She was watching him fall again. Again. Nate's face was contorted in fear, in absolute horror, and she knew that it was because he was looking down at the ground and how far away it was and knowing he was about to die. His arms and legs flailed for purchase against the air. Against nothing. The vision behind him was black, empty, a swirling void of nothing, giving her no clues.

Not the where. Not the when. Not the who or the why.

Only Nate, falling, and every detail of it was so clear she found herself holding her breath, even though she didn't need to breathe here in this vision space, even though she was a nothing presence herself, an incorporeal form. He was falling, and she could hear the sound of the wind whistling through his clothes as he passed, and a desperate scream ripping from his mouth, and all she wanted to do was reach out and catch him.

All she wanted was for him to be safe. But he was falling, falling, falling...

Laura blinked her eyes open on the cell phone, on the message that he hadn't replied to. It was so clear. It was stronger again than the last

167

time. The sound she'd heard, the way he had cried out – even though she'd gained no detail, it had been so strong.

And her head – her head was pounding.

The stronger the headache, the more immediately the vision was going to come true, at least in all of her experience so far. But the concussion – that was new. What if it was skewing the pain? Making it worse?

Was Nate in danger now – like right now?

Or was she getting a false signal?

There was no point in trying to answer the question. It didn't matter. Laura put the car into drive and pulled out of the parking lot, checking the GPS for the route. She had to go to him. She had no choice. If there was even the slightest chance he was in danger, she couldn't leave him to deal with it on his own.

She had no idea where the place she had seen him falling from was, but if she could get to his house, there was a chance he was still there. That she could stop him before he went to whatever location would hold all that danger for him. And in the meantime, she hit dial on Rondelle's number, waiting for it to connect, needing desperately to ask him if Nate was somewhere on a case.

She'd thought that the ebb and wane of the shadow of death over him every time she thought of telling him about her visions meant that the knowledge of them would keep him safe. But it wasn't true. He was in more danger now than he ever had been before.

There was only one way she could interpret that. Every time she'd thought about telling him the truth, she'd thought about healing the growing rift between them. But she'd left it so late, and then he hadn't been able to deal with it. And the rift had widened all the same.

What the visions were telling her was clear.

Nate was in mortal danger – *so long as she was not with him.*

Even if he didn't want to see her now, even if he never wanted to see her again, she wasn't going to let this happen. She was going to go to him. She had to.

Even if he hated her for the rest of his life, she had to be with him right now – so that he would have a rest of his life to live.

NOW AVAILABLE!

ALREADY TAKEN
(A Laura Frost FBI Suspense Thriller—Book 6)

When victims of a serial killer turn up with a creepy signature left on their foreheads—an ornate, wax seal—FBI Special Agent Laura Frost is plagued with visions of people from past centuries. Is her psychic vision misleading her? Or leading her right into the arms of a killer?

"A MASTERPIECE OF THRILLER AND MYSTERY. Blake Pierce did a magnificent job developing characters with a psychological side so well described that we feel inside their minds, follow their fears and cheer for their success. Full of twists, this book will keep you awake until the turn of the last page."
--Books and Movie Reviews, Roberto Mattos (re Once Gone)

ALREADY TAKEN (A Laura Frost FBI Suspense Thriller) is book #6 in a long-anticipated new series by #1 bestseller and USA Today bestselling author Blake Pierce, whose bestseller Once Gone (a free download) has received over 1,000 five star reviews. The Laura Frost series begins with ALREADY GONE (Book #1).

FBI Special Agent and single mom Laura Frost, 35, is haunted by her talent: a psychic ability which she refuses to face and which she keeps secret from her colleagues. While Laura gets obscured glimpses of what the killer may do next, she must decide whether to trust her confusing gift—or her investigative work.

As Laura inspects the wax seals, she realizes the killer is hinting at something. But what? With her detective skills pulling her one way and her psychic vision another, she is torn. Should she trust what's in front of her?

Or should she trust what her unconscious mind is telling her?

In this twisted game of cat and mouse, there is no room for error.

Because if she gets it wrong, another victim will be next.

A page-turning and harrowing crime thriller featuring a brilliant and tortured FBI agent, the LAURA FROST series is a startlingly fresh mystery, rife with suspense, twists and turns, shocking revelations, and driven by a breakneck pace that will keep you flipping pages late into the night.

Books #6–#9 are also available!

Blake Pierce

Blake Pierce is the USA Today bestselling author of the RILEY PAGE mystery series, which includes seventeen books. Blake Pierce is also the author of the MACKENZIE WHITE mystery series comprising fourteen books; of the AVERY BLACK mystery series comprising six books; of the KERI LOCKE mystery series, comprising five books; of the MAKING OF RILEY PAIGE mystery series comprising six books; of the KATE WISE mystery series, comprising seven books; of the CHLOE FINE psychological suspense mystery comprising six books; of the JESSE HUNT psychological suspense thriller series, comprising nineteen books; of the AU PAIR psychological suspense thriller series, comprising three books; of the ZOE PRIME mystery series, comprising six books; of the ADELE SHARP mystery series, comprising thirteen books, of the EUROPEAN VOYAGE cozy mystery series, comprising four books; of the new LAURA FROST FBI suspense thriller, comprising six books (and counting); of the new ELLA DARK FBI suspense thriller, comprising nine books (and counting); of the A YEAR IN EUROPE cozy mystery series, comprising nine books, of the AVA GOLD mystery series comprising six books (and counting); and of the RACHEL GIFT mystery series, comprising six books (and counting).

An avid reader and lifelong fan of the mystery and thriller genre, Blake loves to hear from you, so please feel free to visit www.blakepierceauthor.com to learn more and stay in touch.

BOOKS BY BLAKE PIERCE

RACHEL GIFT MYSTERY SERIES
HER LAST WISH (Book #1)
HER LAST CHANCE (Book #2)
HER LAST HOPE (Book #3)
HER LAST FEAR (Book #4)
HER LAST CHOICE (Book #5)
HER LAST BREATH (Book #6)

AVA GOLD MYSTERY SERIES
CITY OF PREY (Book #1)
CITY OF FEAR (Book #2)
CITY OF BONES (Book #3)
CITY OF GHOSTS (Book #4)
CITY OF DEATH (Book #5)
CITY OF VICE (Book #6)

A YEAR IN EUROPE
A MURDER IN PARIS (Book #1)
DEATH IN FLORENCE (Book #2)
VENGEANCE IN VIENNA (Book #3)
A FATALITY IN SPAIN (Book #4)

ELLA DARK FBI SUSPENSE THRILLER
GIRL, ALONE (Book #1)
GIRL, TAKEN (Book #2)
GIRL, HUNTED (Book #3)
GIRL, SILENCED (Book #4)
GIRL, VANISHED (Book 5)
GIRL ERASED (Book #6)
GIRL, FORSAKEN (Book #7)
GIRL, TRAPPED (Book #8)
GIRL, EXPENDABLE (Book #9)

LAURA FROST FBI SUSPENSE THRILLER
ALREADY GONE (Book #1)
ALREADY SEEN (Book #2)
ALREADY TRAPPED (Book #3)
ALREADY MISSING (Book #4)

ALREADY DEAD (Book #5)
ALREADY TAKEN (Book #6)

EUROPEAN VOYAGE COZY MYSTERY SERIES
MURDER (AND BAKLAVA) (Book #1)
DEATH (AND APPLE STRUDEL) (Book #2)
CRIME (AND LAGER) (Book #3)
MISFORTUNE (AND GOUDA) (Book #4)
CALAMITY (AND A DANISH) (Book #5)
MAYHEM (AND HERRING) (Book #6)

ADELE SHARP MYSTERY SERIES
LEFT TO DIE (Book #1)
LEFT TO RUN (Book #2)
LEFT TO HIDE (Book #3)
LEFT TO KILL (Book #4)
LEFT TO MURDER (Book #5)
LEFT TO ENVY (Book #6)
LEFT TO LAPSE (Book #7)
LEFT TO VANISH (Book #8)
LEFT TO HUNT (Book #9)
LEFT TO FEAR (Book #10)
LEFT TO PREY (Book #11)
LEFT TO LURE (Book #12)
LEFT TO CRAVE (Book #13)

THE AU PAIR SERIES
ALMOST GONE (Book#1)
ALMOST LOST (Book #2)
ALMOST DEAD (Book #3)

ZOE PRIME MYSTERY SERIES
FACE OF DEATH (Book#1)
FACE OF MURDER (Book #2)
FACE OF FEAR (Book #3)
FACE OF MADNESS (Book #4)
FACE OF FURY (Book #5)
FACE OF DARKNESS (Book #6)

A JESSIE HUNT PSYCHOLOGICAL SUSPENSE SERIES

THE PERFECT WIFE (Book #1)
THE PERFECT BLOCK (Book #2)
THE PERFECT HOUSE (Book #3)
THE PERFECT SMILE (Book #4)
THE PERFECT LIE (Book #5)
THE PERFECT LOOK (Book #6)
THE PERFECT AFFAIR (Book #7)
THE PERFECT ALIBI (Book #8)
THE PERFECT NEIGHBOR (Book #9)
THE PERFECT DISGUISE (Book #10)
THE PERFECT SECRET (Book #11)
THE PERFECT FAÇADE (Book #12)
THE PERFECT IMPRESSION (Book #13)
THE PERFECT DECEIT (Book #14)
THE PERFECT MISTRESS (Book #15)
THE PERFECT IMAGE (Book #16)
THE PERFECT VEIL (Book #17)
THE PERFECT INDISCRETION (Book #18)
THE PERFECT RUMOR (Book #19)

CHLOE FINE PSYCHOLOGICAL SUSPENSE SERIES
NEXT DOOR (Book #1)
A NEIGHBOR'S LIE (Book #2)
CUL DE SAC (Book #3)
SILENT NEIGHBOR (Book #4)
HOMECOMING (Book #5)
TINTED WINDOWS (Book #6)

KATE WISE MYSTERY SERIES
IF SHE KNEW (Book #1)
IF SHE SAW (Book #2)
IF SHE RAN (Book #3)
IF SHE HID (Book #4)
IF SHE FLED (Book #5)
IF SHE FEARED (Book #6)
IF SHE HEARD (Book #7)

THE MAKING OF RILEY PAIGE SERIES
WATCHING (Book #1)
WAITING (Book #2)

LURING (Book #3)
TAKING (Book #4)
STALKING (Book #5)
KILLING (Book #6)

RILEY PAIGE MYSTERY SERIES
ONCE GONE (Book #1)
ONCE TAKEN (Book #2)
ONCE CRAVED (Book #3)
ONCE LURED (Book #4)
ONCE HUNTED (Book #5)
ONCE PINED (Book #6)
ONCE FORSAKEN (Book #7)
ONCE COLD (Book #8)
ONCE STALKED (Book #9)
ONCE LOST (Book #10)
ONCE BURIED (Book #11)
ONCE BOUND (Book #12)
ONCE TRAPPED (Book #13)
ONCE DORMANT (Book #14)
ONCE SHUNNED (Book #15)
ONCE MISSED (Book #16)
ONCE CHOSEN (Book #17)

MACKENZIE WHITE MYSTERY SERIES
BEFORE HE KILLS (Book #1)
BEFORE HE SEES (Book #2)
BEFORE HE COVETS (Book #3)
BEFORE HE TAKES (Book #4)
BEFORE HE NEEDS (Book #5)
BEFORE HE FEELS (Book #6)
BEFORE HE SINS (Book #7)
BEFORE HE HUNTS (Book #8)
BEFORE HE PREYS (Book #9)
BEFORE HE LONGS (Book #10)
BEFORE HE LAPSES (Book #11)
BEFORE HE ENVIES (Book #12)
BEFORE HE STALKS (Book #13)
BEFORE HE HARMS (Book #14)

Made in the USA
Middletown, DE
05 April 2022

63706577R00106